I0520189

STORIES MY GRANDMOTHER TOLD ME

Vada Frye Tales - Part 2

(A companion to Part 1: Vada Frye's Ghosts in the Darkness of Despair)

By

J. Wayne Frye

Notice:
This book is written in Canadian English
and teachers should alert their students
to the variances in spellings.

TALES MY GRANDMOTHER TOLD ME

TO:

My long gone <u>grandmother (Vada Cranford Frye)</u>, who was a ray of sunshine in an often gloomy world where dark shadows haunted me as a young boy and a young man. Still, she prepared me for life by sharing tales few other grandmothers would have shared. Why? Because she knew that life was a struggle, and that those who expect the normal fairy tale outcome of "and they lived happily ever after" will be ill prepared for real life.

Also, as always, to my muse:
<u>Lynton Globa Viñas</u> – the dynamic dynamo.

Catalogue Number: 971390-2019

ISBN: 978-1-928183-42-6

Fireside Books – Canadian Division
Part of the Peninsula Publishing Consortium

J. WAYNE FRYE

TALES MY GRANDMOTHER TOLD ME

Table of Contents

TALES MY GRANDMOTHER TOLD ME

About the Author

Wayne Frye's *Aaron Adams* mysteries, *Chablis Louise Chavez* thrillers, *Girl* books and *Lynton* adventures titillate the brains of those who enjoy tantalizing tales of mystery. Growing up in the small town of Asheboro, North Carolina, he wrote his first novel at 15, but waited over twenty years before finally submitting it to a publisher. His life, like the heroes he writes about, has been filled with adventure and excitement. He has been a college hockey coach, professor, and at one time, the youngest university president in the USA. Called a marketing genius by the *Los Angeles Times*, he has been a promotional consultant to hockey teams and motion picture companies. He has been cited for his work with inner-city gangs in Los Angeles. A proud Canadian, he lives on Vancouver Island in Ladysmith and Victoria, British Columbia.

Some of the books by J. Wayne Frye
For Young People

Lynton Curls Her Hair
Lynton Walks on Water
Lynton and the Vampire at Tagaytay Manor
Lynton Buys a Cell-Phone and Hears the Voice of Doom
Lynton Viñas and Beowulf Perez in the Taal Inferno
Lynton and the Ghosts in the Mansion on Balete Drive
Lynton Viñas: Shadow in the Darkness
Lynton's South African Adventure
Lynton, the Karoo Vampire and the Jewels of Omar Bin Abi
Lynton and the Stellenbosch Terror
Lynton and the Cape Town Ghost
Lynton and the Haunting of the HMS Wind Dancer
Hockey Mania and the Mystery of Nancy Running Elk
White Meteors and the Ghost of Sue Ann McGee
How Hockey Saved a Jew From the Holocaust
Sammy Sasquatch and the Sts'ailes Star

For Adults

Something Evil in the Darkness at Hopkins House
The Girl Who Said Goodbye for the Last Time
The Girl Who Motivated Murder Most Foul
The Girl Who Stirred up the Whirlwind
The Girl Who Rode into a Storm
Fall From Apocalypse
Armageddon Now
Worth Part 1: Roaring Through Life Like a Comet in the Midnight Sky
Worth Part 2: The Night of Thunder Road
When Jesus Came to Jersey as the Son of Thunder
When Jesus Came to Canada to Lead an Indigenous Rebellion
When Jesus Came to the Black Hills to do the Ghost Dance
Chablis: Avenging Angel for the Forgotten
Chablis and the Terrorist
Pursuit
The Disappearance
The Rectifier: Dance of Death in the Darkness of Retribution

J. WAYNE FRYE

TALES MY GRANDMOTHER TOLD ME

Prologue
Vada Frye Stories

The door to adventure was open.
                    Monsters might be lurking.

I hung on each word spoken.
                    She grimaced without smirking.

The words; they were haunting.
                    My blood pressure was soaring.

The Boogeyman was always daunting.
                    Never a word from her was boring.

She was a storytelling master.
                    How I hung on every word.

My heart beat faster and faster.
                    The excitement was never deferred.

Grandmother, dear grandmother!
                    She enthralled me with each tale.

The moral I waited to discover.
                    She delivered without fail.

As a small child, I would sit enthralled as my
dear grandmother shared stories with me that

titillated my brain cells and developed my grand sense of imagination that would one day make me a writer. It was a golden time before television descended into banal tripe, before video games that dulled the mind and long before people buried their heads in cell phones rather than communicate with each other on a more personal level. It was a time when children played outside, inventing games rather than sitting in front of screens and playing games with animated creatures developed by corporate robots intent on driving commerce rather than developing inquiring minds. I lived in a world that has faded now, a world of adventure and excitement, a world where the power of storytelling was still an art form practiced by people who had lived without electricity, without television, even without indoor plumbing. These were people who practiced an oral tradition of storytelling that made the imagination soar and reached the innermost child that is deep within us all. How wonderful it was to have an imagination, and to believe in good and evil fairies, to believe in many things you knew were mostly impossible. Yet, it was a time that people my age reflect on with nostalgic delight, a time that is as Margaret Mitchell said, "gone with the wind."

Herein, I am sharing some of the tales my grandmother used to mesmerize me so many years ago. These are not the usual tales, but rather come mostly from the dark side. So, sit back, relax and delve into a fairytale land that will delight, will cause, in some cases, tears and some may even make you sleep with the lights on.

TALES MY GRANDMOTHER TOLD ME

Chapter 1
The Prince with the Nine Sorrows

Eight white peahens went down to the gate.
"Wait!" they said, "little sister, wait!"
They covered her up with feathers so fine;
None went out, when there they became nine.

A long time ago there lived a king and a queen, who had an only son. As soon as he was born his mother gave him to a forester's wife to be nursed; for she herself had to wear her crown all day and had no time for nursing. The forester's wife had just given birth to a daughter of her own; but she loved both children equally and nursed them together like twins.

One night the queen had a dream that made half of her hair turn grey. She dreamed that she saw the prince, her son at the age of twenty, lying dead with a hole where his heart once was; and near him his foster-sister was standing, with a royal crown on her head and his heart bleeding between her hands.

The next morning the queen sent in great haste for the family fairy, and told her of the dream. The fairy said, "This can have but one meaning, and it is an evil one. There is some danger that threatens your son's life in his twentieth year, and his foster-sister is to be the cause of it; also, it seems she is to make herself queen. But leave her to me, and I will avert the evil chance; for the dream coming beforehand shows that the fates mean that he should be saved."

The queen said, "Do anything; only do not destroy the forester's wife's child, for, as yet at least, she has done no wrong. Let her only be carried away to a safe place and made secure and treated well. I will not have my son's happiness grow out of another one's grave."

The fairy said, "Nothing is so safe as a grave when it comes to arresting fate. Still, despite misgivings, I will make everything quite safe within reason, and leave you a clean conscience."

The little prince and the forester's daughter grew up together until they were a year old; then, one day, when their nurse came to look for them, the prince was found, but his foster-sister was lost; and though the search for her was long, she was never seen again, nor could any trace of her be found.

The baby prince pined and pined, and was so sorrowful over her loss that it was feared for a time that he was going to die. But his foster-mother, in spite of her grief over her own child's disappearance, nursed him so well and loved him so much that after a while he recovered his strength. Then the forester's wife gave birth to another daughter, as if to console herself for the loss of the first. But the same night that the child was born the queen had just the same dream over again. She dreamed that she saw her son lying dead at the age of twenty; and there was the hole in his breast, and the forester's daughter was standing by with his heart in her hand and a royal crown upon her head. Again, the queen was terrified.

The queen's hair had gone even greyer, and she sent again for the family fairy, and told her how the dream had repeated itself. The fairy gave her the same advice as before, quieting her fears, and assuring her that however persistent the fates might be in threatening the prince's life, all in the end should be well.

Before another year passed the second of the forester's daughters disappeared, and the prince and his foster-mother cried themselves ill over a loss that had been so cruelly renewed. The queen, seeing how great was the sorrow, and the love that the prince bore for his foster-sisters, began to doubt in her heart and say, "What have I done? Have I saved my son's life by taking away his heart?"

Almost every year the same thing took place, the forester's wife giving birth to another daughter, and the queen on the very same night having the same fearful dream of the fate that threatened her beloved son until, as always the family fairy would come, and then later the wife's child would disappear within a year and be heard of no more.

At last, when nine total daughters in all had been born to the forester's wife and ultimately lost to her when they were but a year old, the queen fell very ill. Every day she grew weaker and weaker, and the dutiful prince forlornly came and sat by her, holding her hand and looking at her with a sorrowful face. At last one night (it was just a year after the last of the forester's children had disappeared) she woke, screamed "the dream, the dream" and died.

The prince was the very saddest of mortals. He said that there were nine sorrows hidden in his heart, of which he could not get rid; and that at night, when all the birds went home to roost, he heard cries of lamentation and pain; but whether these came from very far away, or out of his own heart he could not tell. Yet he grew into manhood and had such grace and tenderness in his nature that all who saw him loved him. His foster-mother, when he spoke to her of his nine sorrows, tried to comfort him, calling him her own nine joys; and, indeed, he was all the joy left in life for her.

When the prince neared his twentieth year, the king, his natural father, felt that he, himself, was becoming old and weary of life and said, "I shall not live much longer, as I can feel the call of death. Very soon my son will be left alone in the world. It is right, therefore, now that he should know of the danger ahead that threatens his life, because he has never been told of the perils in the dreams of the queen."

The old king knew of the prince's nine sorrows, and often he tried to believe that they came by chance, and had nothing to do with the secret that sat at the root of his son's life. But now he feared more and more to tell the prince the story of those nine dreams, lest the knowledge should indeed serve but as the crowning point of his sorrows and break his heart. Yet there was so much danger in leaving the thing untold that at last he summoned the prince to his bedside, meaning to tell him all. The king had worn himself so ill with anxiety and

J. WAYNE FRYE

grief in thinking over the matter that now to tell all was the only means of saving the young prince's life.

The prince came and knelt down, and leaned his head on his father's pillow; and the king delicately whispered into his ear the story of the dreams, and of how for his sake all the prince's foster-sisters had been spirited away. Before his tale was done he could no longer bear to look into his son's face, but closed his eyes, and, with long silences between, spoke in measured tones. When he had ended the discourse, he lay quite still, and the prince kissed his closed eyelids and went softly out of the room.

"Now I know," he said to himself; "now at last," as he came through the woods and knocked at his foster-mother's door. "Other mother," he said to her, "give me a kiss for each of my sisters, for now I am going out into the world to find them, to be rid of the sorrows in my heart."

"They can never be found!" she cried, but she kissed him nine times. "And this," she said, "was Monica, and this was Ponica, and this was Veronica," and so she went over every name. "But now they are only names," she offered through streaming tears.

He went far and wide searching for clues of their whereabouts, until he came upon an old peasant who asked of him, "Where may you be going, fair sir?"

"Truly," answered the prince, "I do not know how far or whither I am going, for I am trying to fill a void in my heart."

The bewildered peasant said, "I wish you well in filling that hole."

The next day as the dark night descended, he came upon a man chopping trees for firewood, who said to him, "Where to so fast? Here the night is so dark and the way so dangerous, one like you should not go alone."

"Nay, I know nothing of this place," said the prince, "only I feel like I am wandering in a foreign land, lost in search of those whom I love."

The woodcutter escorted him through the dark woods to an inn where he spent the night. The next morning he started on journey after journey in search of his lost foster-sisters. After many days he came to a small long valley rich in woods and also where a river with cascading waterfalls brightened a tranquil valley. However, the road ended in the village, and there was no way out but back the way he came. It seemed like the world's end, a place unknown or forgotten, with mostly older inhabitants. Just at the end of the valley, where the woods opened into clear slopes and hollows towards the west, he saw before him, low and overgrown, the walls of a little tumbled-down grange. "There," he said to himself, "I can find shelter for tonight. Never have I felt so tired or such a pain in my heart!"

Before long he came to a gate, and a winding path leading in among lawns and trees to the door of an old house. The house seemed to have been once lived in, but there was no sign of any life now. He pushed open the door, and suddenly there was a sharp rustling of feathers, and nine white female peahens rose up from the ground and flew out of the window into the garden.

The prince searched the whole house over, and found it a mere ruin; the only signs of life to be seen were the white feathers that lifted and blew about over the floors. Outside, the garden was gathering itself together in the dusk, and the peahens were stepping daintily about the lawns, pecking here and there between the blades of grass. They seemed to suit the gentle sadness of the place, which had an air of grief that had grown at ease with itself. The prince went out into the garden and walked about among the quietly stepping birds, but they took no heed of him. They came picking up their food between his very feet, as though he were not there. Silence held all the air, and in the cleft of the valley the day drooped to its end. Just before it grew dark, the nine white peahens gathered together at the foot of a great elm, and lifting up their throats they wailed miserably in chorus. Their lamentable cry touched the prince's heart; "Where," he asked himself, "have I heard such sorrow before?" Then, all with one accord, the birds sprang rustling up to the lowest boughs of the elm and settled themselves to roost.

The prince went back to the house to find some corner amid its half-ruined rooms to sleep in. But there the air was putrid, and an unpleasant smell of moisture came from the floor and walls. So, the night being warm, he returned to the garden, and folding himself in his cloak lay down under the tree where the nine peahens were roosting.

For a long time he tried to sleep, but could not, because there was so much pain and sorrow in his heart. Presently, when it was close upon midnight, over his head one of the birds stirred and ruffled through all its feathers, and he heard a soft voice say, "Sisters are you awake?"

All the other peahens lifted their heads, and turned towards the one that had spoken, saying, "Yes, sister, we are awake."

Then the first one said, "Our brother is here."

They all said, "He is our enemy; it is for him that we endure this sorrow."

"Tonight," said the first, "we may all be free."

They answered, "Yes, we may all be free! Who will go down and peck out his heart? Then we shall be free."

And the first who had spoken said, "I will go down!"

"Do not fail, sister!" said all the others. "For if you fail you can speak to us no more."

The first peahen answered, "Do not fear that I shall fail!" And she began stepping down the long boughs of the elm.

The prince lying below heard all that was said. "Ah, poor sisters," he thought, "have I found you at last; and are all these sorrows brought upon you for me?" And he unloosed his shirt, and opened it wide, making his breast bare for the peahen to come and peck out his heart. He lay still with his eyes shut, and when she reached the ground the peahen found him lying there, as it seemed to her fast asleep with his breast bare for the stroke of her beak.

Then so fair he looked to her, and so gentle in his youth, that she had pity on him, and stood weeping by his side, and laying her head against his, whispered, "Oh brother, once we lay as babes together and were nursed at the same breast! How can I peck out your heart?"

Then she stole softly back into the tree, and crouched down again by her companions. They said to her, "Our minute of midnight is nearly gone. Is there blood on your beak! Have you our brother's heart for us?" But the other answered never a word.

In the morning the peahens rustled down out of the elm, and went about grazing. To the prince they showed no sign either of hatred or fear, but went to and fro carelessly, pecking at the ground about his feet. Only one came with drooping head and wings and sleeked itself to his caress, until the prince, stooping down, whispered in her ear, "Oh sister, why did you not peck out my heart?" She did not reply.

At night, as before, the peahens all cried in chorus as they went up into the elm, and the prince came and wrapped himself in his cloak and lay down at the foot of it to watch. At midnight eight peahens lifted their heads, and said, "Sister, why did you fail last night?" But their sister gave them not a word.

"Alas!" they said, "now she has failed. Unless one of us succeeds, we shall never hear her speak with her human voice again. Why is it that you weep so," they said, "now that deliverance is so near?"

The poor peahen was shaken with weeping, and her tears fell down in loud drops upon the ground. Then the next sister said, "I will go down! He is asleep. I will not fail!"

So she climbed softly down the tree, and the prince opened his shirt and laid his breast bare for her to come and take out his heart. Presently she stood by his side, and when she saw him she too had pity for the youth. She shut her eyes, and lifted her head for the stroke, but then weakness seized her, and she laid her head softly upon his heart and said, "Once the breast that gave me milk gave milk also to you. You were my sister's brother, and she spared you. How can I peck out your heart?" And having said this she went softly back into the tree, and crouched down among her sisters.

They said to her, "Have you blood upon your beak? Is his heart ours?" But she answered them not a word.

The next day the two sisters, who because their hearts betrayed them had become absolutely mute, followed the prince wherever he went, and stretched up their heads to his caresses as they pranced about with him the entire day. But the others went and came indifferently, careless except for food, for until midnight their human hearts were asleep.

That night the same thing happened as before. "Sisters," said the youngest, "tonight I will go down, since the two eldest of us have failed. My wrong is fresher in my heart than theirs! Be sure I shall not fail!"

So the youngest peahen came down from the tree, and the prince laid his heart bare for her beak, but the bird could not find the will to peck it out. And so it was the next night, and the next, until eight nights were gone. So at last, only one sole peahen was left to perform the deed. At midnight she raised her head, saying, "Sisters are you awake?"

They all turned, and gazed at her while they were weeping, but could say no words. Then she said, "You have all failed, having all tried but me. Now if I fail we shall remain mute and captive forever, more undone by the loss of our last remaining gift of speech than we were at first. But I tell you, dear sisters, I will not fail, for the happiness of you all lies with me now!"

Then she went softly down the tree; and one by one they all went following her, and weeping, to see what the end would be. They stood some way apart, watching with upturned heads, as the last of the sisters came and stood by the prince. Then she, too, looked at him, and saw his breast made bare for her beak; and the love of him went deep down into her heart. And she tried and tried to shut her eyes and deal the stroke, but could not.

She trembled and sighed, and turned to look at her sisters, where they all stood weeping silently together. "They have spared him," she said to herself: "why should not I do the same?"

But the Prince, seeing that she, too, was about to fail like the rest of them, turned and said, as if in his sleep, "Come, come, little peahen and peck out my heart!"

At that she turned back again to him, and laid her head down upon his heart and cried more sadly than those had before her. Then he said, "You have eight sisters, and a mother who cries for her children to return!"

Yet, still she thought he was dreaming and speaking only in his sleep. The other peahens came no nearer, but stood weeping silently. She looked from him to them. "Oh," she cried, "I have a wicked heart to let one stand in the way of nine!" Then she threw up her neck and cried lamentably, wishing that the prince would wake up, see her and so escape. And at that all the other peahens lifted up their heads and wailed with her, but the prince never turned, nor lifted a finger, nor uttered a sound.

Then she drew in a deep breath, and closed her eyes fast. "Let my sisters go, but let me be as I am!" she cried; and with that she stooped down, and pecked out his heart.

All her sisters shrieked as their human shapes returned to them. "Oh, sister! Oh, wicked little sister!" they cried, "What have you done?"

The little white peahen crouched close down to the side of the dead prince. "I loved him more than you all!" she tried to say, but she only lifted her head and wailed again and again.

The prince's heart lay beating at her feet, so glad to be rid of its nine sorrows that mere joy made it live on, though all the rest of the body lay cold, as the peahen leaned down upon the prince's breast, and there wailed without ceasing such a sullen moan that tree limbs bowed downward in sorrow.

J. WAYNE FRYE

Suddenly, piercing with her beak her own breast, she drew out her own living heart and laid it in the place where his had been. And, as she did so, the wound where she had pierced him closed and became healed, and her heart was, as it were, buried in the prince's breast. In her death agony she could feel it there, her own heart leaping within his breast for joy.

The prince, who had seemed to be dead, flushed from head to foot as the warmth of life came back to him. With one deep breath he woke, and found the little white peahen lying as if dead between his arms. Then he laughed softly and rose (his goodness making him wise), and taking up his own still beating heart he laid it into the place of hers. At the first beat of it within her breast, the peahen became transformed as all her sisters had been, and her own human form came back to her as the pain and the wound in her breast grew healed, so that she stood up alive and well in the prince's arms.

Then all around was so much embracing and happiness that it is out of reach for tongue or pen to describe. For truly the prince and his foster-sisters loved each other well, and could put no bounds upon their contentment. As for the prince and the one who had plucked out his heart, of no two was the saying ever more truly told that they had lost their hearts to each other; nor was ever love in the world known before that carried with it such harmony as theirs. So, it all came about according to the queen's dream so many years before.

The forester's daughter wore the royal crown upon her head, and long before the old king died he realized his wife's dream had not been a nightmare after all. Rather, it was the foretelling of a grand union between two who would lead the kingdom for many years, and the nine sorrows borne by the prince were no longer sorrows but great joy.

TALES MY GRANDMOTHER TOLD ME

Chapter 2
Evil Sometimes Wins in the End

Life is made of distant springs and falls.
A straight route is not what you own.

A long time ago there lived a king and a queen
who loved each other dearly. They had both fallen
in love at first sight; and as their love began so it
went on through all their lives. Yet, this which
was the cause of all their happiness was the cause
also of all their misfortunes.

In his youth, when he was a beautiful young
bachelor, the king had the ill-luck to attract the
heart of a jealous and powerful fairy; and though
he never gave her the least bit of hope or
encouragement, when she heard that his love had
been won at first sight by a mere mortal, her rage
and resentment knew no bounds. She said nothing,
however, but bided her time for revenge.

After they had been married a year, the queen
presented her husband with a daughter, and before
she was yet a day old she was the most beautiful
object in the world, and life seemed to promise her
nothing but good fortune and happiness.

The kind family fairy came to the blessing of the
new-born; and she, looking at the child as it lay
beautifully asleep in its cradle, and seeing that it
had beauty and health, promised it love as the next
best gift it was within her power to offer. The
queen, who knew how much happiness her own
love had brought her, embraced the fairy and gave
her thanks for the promise.

Suddenly, a crow landed on the window sill and it said in the aggrieved evil fairy's voice "I will give her love at first sight! The first living thing that appears before her she shall love to distraction, whether it be man or monster, prince or pauper, bird, beast or reptile." The good fairy then waved menacingly at the crow, and it flittered away into the sky.

Up through the boards of the floor, and out from under the bed, and in through the window, came a crowd of all the ugliest things in the world. Thick and fast they came, gathering about the cradle and lifting their heads over the edge of it, waiting for the poor little princess to wake up and fall in love at first sight with one of them.

Luckily, the child was asleep, and the good fairy said they should take the princess into a dark room where no glimmer of light could get in. She turned to the queen and said, "Till I can devise a better way, keep her in the dark, and when you take her into the open air you must blindfold her eyes. Some day, when she is of a fit age, I will bring a handsome prince for her, and only to him shall you un-blindfold her, and make love safe for her."

She went away then, leaving the king and queen deeply stricken with grief over the harm which had befallen their daughter. They did not dare to present even themselves before her eyes lest love for them, fatal and consuming, should drive her into obsessive love for her parents.

In utter darkness, over the years the queen would sit and cherish her daughter, clasping her to her breast, and calling her by all sweet names, but the little face, except when it was sound asleep, she never dared to see, nor did the baby-princess know the face of the mother who loved her.

By and by, however, the good fairy came again, saying, "Now, I have a plan by which your child may enjoy the delights of seeing, and no ill come of it. You see, the evil crow said a living person. Thus, the image of a person is not living."

And she caused to be made a large chamber, the whole of one side of which was a mirror. High up in the opposite wall were windows and across on to the mirror came all the sweet sights of the world from outside, glimpses of wood and field, and the sun, the moon and the stars and of every bird as it flew by. So, the little princess sat in a place looking towards the mirror, and there her eyes learned gradually all the beautiful things of the world. In the glass before her, she learned to know her mother's face, and to love it dearly in a gentle child-like fashion, and when she could talk she became very wise, understanding all that was told her about the danger of looking at anything alive, except by its reflection in the glass.

When she went out into the open air, she always wore a bandage over her eyes, lest she should look and love something too well, but in the chamber of the mirror her eyes were free to see whatever they could. The good fairy, making herself invisible, came and taught her to read, make music, draw and converse intelligently.

By the time she was eighteen she was charming, accomplished, and incredibly beautiful. Thus, the good fairy went away to fetch the ideal prince.

TALES MY GRANDMOTHER TOLD ME

The very day after the fairy had left on her quest, as the morning was fine, the princess went out with one of her maids for a walk through the woods. Over her patient eyes she wore a bandage of green silk, through which she felt the sunlight fall pleasantly.

Out of doors the Princess knew most things by their sounds. She passed under rustling leaves, and along by the side of running water, and at last she heard the silence of the water, and knew that she was standing by the great fish-pond in the middle of the wood. Then she said to her companion, "Is there not some great bird fishing out there, for I hear the dipping of his bill, and the water falling off it as he draws out the fish?"

And just as she was saying that, the wicked fairy from long ago, who had long bided her time, coming softly up from behind, pushed the companion off the bank into the deep water of the pond. Then she snatched away the silk bandage, and before the princess had time to think or close her eyes, she had lost her heart to a great heron that was standing half-way up to his feathers fishing among the reeds.

The princess, with her eyes set free, swooned at the sight of him. She stretched out her arms and cried for the bird to come to her, and he came in stately fashion and settled down on the bank beside her. She drew his slender neck against her white throat, and laughed and cried with her arms round him, loving him, ignoring her companion who was struggling to get out of the water, because all she cared for now was the heron.

J. WAYNE FRYE

The heron looked gravely at her with kind eyes, and bird-like, gave her all the love he could in a mere gaze, until casting his grey wings about, lifted himself and sailed slowly back to his fishing among the reeds.

The companion had crawled out of the water, and stood wringing her clothes and her hands beside the princess. "Oh, sweet mistress," she cried, with lamentation, "now all the evil has come about, which it was our whole aim to avoid! And what will the queen say?"

But the Princess answered, smiling, "Foolish girl, I had no thought of what happiness meant till now! See you where my love is gone? Did you notice the bend of his neck and the exceeding length of his legs, and the stretch of his grey wings as he flew? This pond is his hall of mirrors, wherein he sees the reflection of his entire world. Surely I, from my hall of mirrors, am the true mate for him!"

Her maid, seeing how far the evil had gone, and that no worse could now happen, ran back to the palace and curdled all with tales of what had occurred. The king and the queen rushed down, and there they found the princess with the heron once more in her arms, kissing and fondling it with all the marks of a sweet and maidenly passion. "Dear mother," she said, as soon as she saw the queen, "the happiness, which you feared would be sorrow, has come; and it is such joy I have no name for it. I am in love. How sweet it is! I can now see all the world with my own eyes and you also at last!"

For the first time in her life she kissed her mother's face in the full light of day. But her mother hung sobbing upon her neck, "Oh, my darling, my dear daughter" she wept, "does your heart belong forever to this grey bird?"

Her daughter answered, "He is more than all the world to me! Look upon him? Consider the bend of his neck, the length of his legs, and the waving of his wings; his skill also when he fishes; what imagination, what presence of mind!"

"Alas, alas," sorrowed the queen, "dear daughter, is this all true to you?"

"Mother," cried the princess, clinging to her, "is the entire world blind but for me?"

The heron had become quite fond of the princess over time; wherever she went it followed her, and, indeed, without it nowhere would she go. Whenever it was near her, the princess laughed and sang, and when it was out of her sight she became dark and gloomy as a cloudy night.

When the good family fairy came (for she was at once sent for by the forlorn queen, and told of all that had happened), she said with deep conviction, "Dear Madam, there are but two things you can do: either you can wring the heron's neck, and leave the princess to die of grief, or you can make the princess happy in her own way by accepting her love for this creature. At her birth I gave your daughter love for my gift; now it is hers, will you let her keep it?"

The queen looked harshly at the fairy and said, "You want us to not take this despicable love from her. Let her keep it?"

J. WAYNE FRYE

"There is but one way to rectify this," answered the fairy.

"Do not tell me the way," said the queen weeping, "only let the way be, because all I want is for my daughter to be happy!"

So they forlornly went with the fairy down to the great pond, and there sat the princess, with the grey heron against her heart. She smiled as she saw them coming. "I see good in your hearts towards me!" she cried. "Dear fairy, give me the thing that I want, that my love may be happy and carefree."

Then the fairy stroked her but once with her wand, and she became a grey female heron. The two grey herons suddenly rose up from the bank, and sailed away to a hiding-place in the reeds. The fairy said to the queen, "You have made your daughter happy; and still she will have her voice and her human heart, and will remember you with love and gratitude; but her greatest love will be for the grey heron and her home among the reeds."

So the changed life of the princess began; every day her mother went down to the pool and called, and the princess came rising up out of the reeds, and folded her grey wings over her mother's heart. Every day her mother said, "Daughter of mine are you happy?"

The princess answered her. "Yes, for I love and am loved."

Yet, each time the mother heard more and more of a note of sadness come her daughter's voice; and at last one day she said, "Answer me truly, as the mother who brought you into the world, whether you are happy in your heart of hearts or not?"

The heron-princess laid her sorrowful head upon the lovingly sympathetic queen's heart, letting out a long, forlorn sigh and said, "Mother, my heart is breaking with love!"

"For who, then?" asked the astonished queen.

"For my grey heron, which I love, and who loves me so much. And yet it is love that divides us, for I am still troubled with a human heart, and often it aches with sorrow, because all the love in it can never be fully understood or shared by my heron, and I have my human voice left, and that gives me a hundred things to say all day, for which there is no word in heron's language, and so he cannot understand them. Therefore, these things only make a gulf between him and me. For all the other grey herons there is happiness, but not for me who has too big a heart between my wings."

Her mother said softly, "Wait, wait, little heron-daughter, and it shall be well with you!" Then she went to the fairy and said, "My daughter's heart is lonely among the reeds, for the grey heron's love covers but half of it. Give her some companions of her own kind that her hours may become merry again!"

So the fairy summoned the princess's former maids and turned five of them into herons, and sent them down to the pool. The five herons stood each on one leg in the shallows of the pool, and cried all day long; and their tears fell down into the water and frightened away the fish that came their way, for they had human hearts that cried out to be let go. "Oh, cruel, cruel," they wept, whenever the heron-princess approached, "see what we suffer because of you, and what has been made of us for your sake!"

The princess came to her mother and said, "Dear mother, take them away, for their crying wearies me, and the pool is bitter with their tears! They bring me sadness, rather than joy, for they are not happy as herons."

Her mother said, "It is my coming every day also that keeps the sorrow within you, for you still cling to me and my love."

The princess answered with great conviction, "This sorrow belongs to my birthright; you must still come; but for the others, let the fairy take them away."

So the fairy came and released the five maids whom she had changed into herons. And they came up out of the water, stripping themselves of their grey feather-skins and throwing them back into the pool. The fairy said, "You foolish maids, you have thrown away a gift that you should have valued; these skins you could have kept and held as heirlooms in your families."

The five maids answered, "We want to forget that there are such things as herons in the world!"

After much thought the queen said to the fairy, "You have changed a princess into a heron and five maids into herons and back again; cannot you change one heron into a prince?"

The fairy answered sadly, "My power has limits; I can bring down, but I cannot bring up, if there be no heart to answer our call. The five maids only followed their hearts that were human when I called them back, but a heron has only a heron's heart, and unless its heart becomes too great for a bird and he can earn a human one, I cannot change him to a higher form."

"How can he earn a human one?" asked the queen. "Only if he loves the princess so well that his love for her becomes stronger than his life," answered the fairy. "Then he will have earned a human body, and then I can give him the form that his heart suits best. There may be a chance if we wait for it and are patient, for the princess's love is great and may work miracles."

A little while after this, the queen watching, saw that the two herons (daughter and mate) were making a nest among the reeds. "What have you there?" said the mother to her daughter.

"A little hollow place," answered the heron-princess, "and in it the moon lies."

A little while after the queen said, "And what have you there, now, little daughter?"

Her daughter answered, "Only a small hollow space; but in it two moons lie."

The queen told the family fairy how in a hollow of the reeds laid two moons. Then the fairy offered the queen some joy, "Now," said the fairy, "we will wait no longer. If your daughter's love has touched the heron's heart and made it grow larger than a bird's, I can help them both to happiness; but if not, then birds they must still remain."

Among the reeds the heron said in bird language to his wife, "Go and stretch your wings for a little while over the water; it is weary work to wait here so long in the reeds." The heron-princess looked at him with her bird's eyes, and all the human love in her heart strove to make itself known. Also her tongue was full of the longing to utter sweet words, but she kept them back, knowing they were beyond the heron's power to understand. So she answered merely in heron's language, "Come with me."

They rose, wing beating beside wing; and the reflection of their grey breasts slid out under them over the face of the water. Higher they went and higher, passing over the tree tops, and keeping time together as they flew. All at once the wings of the grey heron flagged, then took a deep beat, as he cried to the heron-princess, "Turn, and go home, yonder there is danger flying to meet us!"

Before them hung a brown blot in the air, that winged forward and grew larger. The two herons turned and flew back. "Rise," cried the grey heron, "we must rise!"

The princess knew what was behind, and struggled with all the strength of her wings for escape. The grey heron was bearing ahead on stronger wings.

"With me, with me!" he cried. "If it gets above us, one of us is dead!" But the falcon had fixed his eyes on the princess for his quarry, and flew furiously toward her.

He was fast and swift, and she was slow and lumbering. She flapped her wings with great intent, but she could not keep up with her mate as the falcon gained and gained on her.

The grey heron swung back to her side; she saw the anguish and fear of his upward glance as his head swiftly moved by hers. Past her the falcon went, towering for the final deadly swoop.

The princess cried in heron's language, "Farewell, dear mate." But the grey heron only kept closer to her side.

Overhead the falcon closed in its wings and fell like a dead weight out of the clouds. "Drop!" cried the grey heron to his mate and at his word she dropped; but he stayed, stretching up his wings, and, passing between the descending falcon and its prey, caught in his own body the death-blow from its beak. Drops of his blood fell from above upon the heron-princess.

He, stricken in body; she in soul, together they fell down to the margin of the pool. The falcon still clung fleshing its beak in the neck of its prey. The heron-princess threw back her head, and, darting furiously, struck her own sharp bill deep into the falcon's breast. The bird threw out its wings with a hoarse cry and fell toward the ground dead, with a little tuft of the grey heron's feathers still upon its beak.

The heron-princess crouched down in great sorrow, and covered with her wings the dying form of her loving mate. In her sorrow she spoke to him in her own tongue, forgetting her bird's language.

The grey heron lifted his head, and, gazing up tenderly, answered her with a human voice: "Dear wife," he said, "at last I have the happiness so long denied to me of giving utterance in the speech that is your own because of the love that you have put into my heart. Often I have heard you speak and have not understood; now something has touched my heart, and changed it, so that I can both speak and understand."

"Beloved," she said as she laid her head down by his. "The ends of the world belong to us now. Lie down, and die gently by my side, and I will die with you, filling my heart with happiness that I have loved you and been loved by you.

"No," said the grey heron, "do not die yet! Remember the two little moons that lie in the hollow among the reeds." Then he laid his head down by hers, being too weak to say more.

They folded their wings over each other, and closed their eyes without knowing that the fairy was standing by them, until she stroked them both softly with her wand, saying to each of them the same words: "Human hearts and human forms, come out of the herons."

And out came two human forms; the one was the princess restored again to her own shape, but the other was a beautiful youth, with a bird-like look about the eyes and long slender limbs. The princess, as she gazed on him, found hardly any change, for love remained the same, binding him close to her heart; and, grey heron or beautiful youth, he was all one to her now, as her love was pure.

Then came the queen, weeping for joy, and embracing them both, and after them, the fairy. "Oh, how good an ending," she cried, "has come to a terrible dream."

J. WAYNE FRYE 33

As the queen began to lead the way back to the palace, the youth turned and took up the two heron skins which he and his wife had let fall, and followed, carrying them upon his arm. And as they came past the bed of reeds, the princess went aside, and, stooping down in a certain place drew out from thence something which she came carrying, softly wrapped in the folds of her gown.

With what rejoicing, the princess and her husband were welcomed by the king and all the court. For a whole month the festivities continued; and whenever she showed herself, there was the princess sitting with two eggs in her lap, and her hands over them to keep them warm. The king was impatient. "Why cannot you send them down to the poultry yard to be hatched?" he said.

But the princess replied smiling, "My moons are my own, and I will keep them to myself."

"Do you hear?" she said one day, at last; and everybody who listened could hear something going "tap, tap," inside the shells. Presently the eggs cracked, and out of each, at the same moment, came a little grey heron.

When she saw that they were herons, the queen wrung her hands. "Oh fairy," she cried, "What a disappointment is this! I had hoped two babies would come out of the shells."

The fairy said, "It is no matter. Half of their hearts are human already; birds' hearts do not beat so. If you wish it, I can change them." So she stroked them softly with her wand, saying to each, "Human hearts and human forms come out into the world."

Yet she had to stroke them three times before they would turn; and she said to the princess, "My dear, you were too satisfied with your lot when you laid your moon-children. I doubt if more than a quarter of them is human."

"I was very satisfied," said the princess, and she smiled at her husband.

At last, however, on the third stroke of the wand, the heron's skins dropped off, and they changed into a pair of very small babies, a boy and a girl. But the difference between them and other children was that instead of hair their heads were covered with a fluff of downy grey feathers. Also, they had queer, round, bird-like eyes and were able to sleep standing.

Now, after this the happiness of the princess was great; but the fairy said to her, "Do not let your husband see the heron-skins again for some while, lest the memory for his old life should return to him and take him away from you. Only by exchange with another can he ever get back his human form again, if he surrenders it of his own free will. And who is there so poor that he would willingly give up his human form to become a bird?"

So the princess took the four heron skins, her own and her husband's and her two children's, and hid them away in a closet of which only she had the key.

She wore the key around her neck every day and night. Finally, her dear husband asked "What is that little key that you wear always hung round your neck?

She answered him, "It is the key to your happiness and mine. Do not ask more than that!" At that there was a look on his face that made her say, "You are happy, are you not?"

He replied, smiling with glee, "Happy indeed. Yes."

Yet, though indeed he told no untruth, and was happy whenever she was with him, there were times when a restlessness and a longing for wings took hold of him; for, as yet, the life of a man was new and half strange to him, and a taint of his old life still mixed itself with his blood. But to her he was ashamed to say what might seem a complaint against his great fortune, so when she said "happiness," he thought, "is it just the turning of that key that I want before my happiness can be perfect?"

Therefore, one night when the early season of spring made his longing strong in him, he took the key from the princess while she slept, and opened the little closet in which hung the four feather coats. And when he saw his own, all at once he remembered the great pools of water, and how they lay in the shine and shadow of the moonlight, while the fish rose in rings upon their surface. And at that so great a longing came into him to revisit his old haunts that he reached out his hand and took down the heron-skin from its nail and put it over himself, so that immediately his old life took hold of him, and he flew out of the window in the form of a grey heron.

In the morning, the princess found the key gone from her neck, and her husband's place empty.

J. WAYNE FRYE

She went in haste to the closet, and there stood the door wide with the key in it, and only three heron-skins hanging where four had used to be.

Then she came crying to the family fairy, "My husband has taken his heron-skin and is gone! Tell me what I can do!"

The fairy pitied her with all her heart, but could do nothing. "Only by exchange," she said, "can he get back his human shape; and who is there so poor that he would willingly lose his own form to become a bird? Only your children, who are but half human, can put their heron-skins on and off as they like and when they like."

In deep grief the princess went to look for her husband down by the pools in the wood. But now his shame and sorrow at having deceived her were so great that as soon as he heard her voice he hid himself among the reeds, for he knew now that, having put on his heron-skin again, he could not take it off unless some one gave him a human form in exchange.

At last, however, so pitiful was the cry of the princess for him that he could bear to hear it no more, so rising up from the reeds he came trailing to her sadly over the water. "Ah, dear love!" she said when he came to her, "if I had not distrusted you, you would not have deceived me. Thus, for my fault we are punished."

So she sorrowed, and he answered her with deep sadness in his aching heart. "It is I who is the deceiver."

He took a long, deep breath and continued with sadness in his voice. "I simply longed for the freedom we once had." I thought I was not happy. Yet, I feared to tell you."

Thus they shared sorrow together, both laying on themselves the blame and the burden. Then, the princess said to him: "Be here for me tonight, for now I must go; but I shall return."

She went back to the palace, and told her mother all that had happened. And now, she said, "you who know where my happiness lies will not forbid me from following it; for my heart is again with the grey heron." The queen wept.

So that night, the princess went and kissed her children as they slept standing up in their beds, with their funny feather-pates to one side, and then she took down her skin of feathers and put it on, and became changed once more into a grey heron. And again she went up to the two in their cots, and kissed their heads saying: "They who can change at will, being but half human, they will come and visit us in the great pool by the wood, and bring back word of what goes on here."

In the morning the princess was gone, and the two children when they woke looked at each other and said, "Did we dream last night?"

They both answered each other, "Yes, first we dreamed that our mother came and kissed us, and we liked that. And then we dreamed that a grey heron came and kissed us, and we liked that better still!" They waved their arms up and down and said, "Why do we not have wings?"

In the palace they would stand on one leg and sigh with their heads on one side; but no one ever saw tears come out of their bird-like eyes. At night they would dream that two grey herons came and stood by their bedsides, kissing them as they were told their parents were away and would return soon. "And where in the world," they said when they woke, "are our wings."

One day, wandering about in the palace, they came upon the closet in which hung the two little feather coats. They opened the closet and with hard bright eyes beaming with recognition, now they knew what they would do. "If we told, they would be taken from us," they said; and they waited until it was night. Then they crept back and took the two little coats from their pegs, and, putting them on, were turned into two young herons.

Through the window they flew, away down to the great fish-pond in the woods. Their father and mother saw them coming, and clapped their wings for joy. "See," they said, "our children have come to visit us. What further happiness can we want?"

All night long the two young herons stayed with their parents; they bathed, and fished, and flew, until they were weary. Then the princess showed them the nest among the reeds, and told them all the story of their lives.

"It is much nicer to be herons than to be real people," said the young ones, sadly, and became very sorrowful when dawn drew on, and their mother told them to go back to the palace and hang up the feather coats again, and be as they had been the day before.

Long the days now seemed to them. They hardly waited until it was night before they took down their feather-skins, and, putting them on, flew out and away to the fish-pond in the woods.

So every night they went, when all in the palace was asleep; and in the morning came back before anyone was astir, and were found by their nurses lying demurely between the sheets, just as they had been left the night before. Then, one day the queen, when she went to see her daughter, said to her, "My child, your two children are growing less like human beings and more like birds every day. Nothing will they learn or do, but stand all day flapping their arms up and down, and saying, where are our wings, where are our wings? Thus, the idea of one of them ever coming to the throne makes your father's hair stand on end under his crown."

"Oh, mother," said the heron-princess, "I have made a sad bed for you and my father to lie on!" Thus, the princess was saddened by the state of affairs caused by her love for the grey heron.

One day the two children said to each other, "Our father and mother are sad, because they want to be real persons again, instead of having wings and catching fish the way we like to do. Let us give up being real persons, which is all so much trouble, and make them exchange with us!"

Yet, when the two young herons went down to the pond and proposed it to them, their parents said, "You are young; you do not know what you would be giving up." Thus, the parents refused to exchange places.

Now, one morning it happened that the child herons were so late in returning to the palace that the queen, coming into their chamber, found the two beds empty; and just as she had turned away to search for them elsewhere, she heard a noise of wings and saw the two young herons come flying in through the window. Then she hid and observed them taking off their feather-skins and hanging them up in the closet, and after that go and lie down in their beds so as to look as if they had been there all night.

The queen struck her hands together with horror at the sight, but she crept away softly, so that they did not know they had been found out. But as soon as they were out of their beds and at play in another part of the palace, the queen went to the closet, and setting fire to the two heron-skins where they hung, burnt them till not a feather was left, and only a heap of grey ashes remained piled high on the floor to indicate what had occurred during the day.

That night, when the children went to the closet and found their skins gone, and saw what had become of them, their grief knew no bounds. They trembled with fear and rage, and tears rained out of their eyes as they beheld themselves deprived of their bird bodies and made into real persons for all-time.

They made themselves quite ill with grief; and that night, for the first time since they had found their way to the closet, they stayed where their nurses had put them, and did not even stand up in their beds to go to sleep. There they lay gasping with grief over the state of things. Presently their father and mother came seeking them, wondering why they had not come down to the fish-pond as they normally did. "Where are my children?" cried the heron-princess, putting her head in through the window.

"Here we are both at death's door!" they cried. "Come and see us die, because our wicked grandmother has burnt our feather-skins and made us into real persons forever and ever, but we will die rather than face life without our cloak of feathers.

The parent herons, when they heard that, flew in through the window and bent down over the little ones' beds. The two children reached up their arms and sadly cried, "Give us your feathers, please. We shall die if you don't, for we do not wish to live if we cannot be birds." Still the parent birds hesitated, for they knew not what to do.

Now the parents had tears in their heron eyes, because seeing their children so sad was breaking their hearts. "Bend down, and let me whisper something!" said the boy to his father.

"Bend down, and let me whisper something to you dear mother!" cried the girl to her mother. Father and mother bent down over the faces of their sick children. Then the children, both together, caught hold of them, and cried "Human heart, and human form, exchange with the grey heron!"

The feather-skins came off and diminished in size, wrapping around the children. At the same time, the parents took human shape as the children turned into herons. The young herons laughed and shouted and clapped their wings for joy.

TALES MY GRANDMOTHER TOLD ME

Still, there was sadness in the hearts of the parents, now in human form, because they were separated from their children not when it came to love, but when it came to human form. Although they loved the heron-children as much as they did when they were in human forms, they wished that it would be possible to share the best of both worlds, but alas, in consultation with the fairy, it was obvious that things could not be altered.

The other sad fact the parents had to face was that herons do not live as long as humans, so they had to simply accept the fact they would, in all likelihood, out-live their children. After extensive research they found that herons lived an average of ten years, so many nights, after watching their children muddle into the reeds and sleep, they sat by the pond side pondering the sad fate that one day their children would die before them, because they were herons. The princess often cried herself to sleep with the sad thoughts of those days that would come far too soon when her heron-children would die. In fact, she cried and cried until finally she died from misery, leaving her husband alone with their heron children.

Within a few months, her husband also died of a broken heart, leaving their heron children all alone. After the death of the two, the king spent many lonely hours sitting by the pond, watching his heron grandchildren play, telling them about their parents and how much they loved each other, whereupon the children cried.

It would be nice to say that all turned out well in the end, but life is not always joyous, and the king one day as he walked to the pond heard screaming. He scurried to see what was causing such alarm, and he dropped to his knees in anguish as he watched two eagles soar into the sky with the heron grandchildren in their mouths. He had lost all. He lay down on the banks of the pond, and sadness overwhelmed him because his wife, his daughter, his son-in-law and grandchildren were all gone now, and despite being king, he had nothing. Even his gold crown he took off and lay on the ground. He sighed and took his last breath, because he realized that without his loved ones his kingdom was an empty place where only sorrow dwelled. The kingdom fell into disarray and the populace scattered, leaving the kingdom to rot and decay. All that was left were the tales from the former residents of how a once prosperous and grand kingdom disappeared into the void of lost hope. Oh, there was one other thing left. Remember that evil fairy that had loved the young bachelor king, and when hearing that his love had been won at first sight by a mere mortal, but bided her time for revenge and appeared as a crow when the princess was born? Well, to this very day when a light breeze blows across that pond, a black crow flies overhead and can be heard laughing at the fate of the king whom she had marked for such horrid revenge. Far too often, in the real world evil wins in the end. And today, when you hear a crow making the sounds "Kaw, Kaw, Kaw," it is the evil fairy laughing.

Chapter 3
Bow Before Their Masters

The person who knows a charlatan
can blatantly expose his chicanery,
but there are people who embrace lies,
and will blindly follow a buffoon.
It is always easier to let someone else
do your thinking for you.

Many years ago, a king died, leaving two sons. One was the child of his first wife, and the other of his second, who surviving him became his widow. When the king was dying he took off the royal crown which he wore, and set it upon the head of the elder born, the son of his first wife, and said to him, "God is the lord of the air, and of the water, and of the dry land, so this gift cometh to thee from God. Be merciful over whatsoever thou holdest power, as God is!" And saying these words he laid his hands upon the heads of his two sons and died.

Now this kingly crown was no ordinary crown, for it was made of the very gold brought by the three Wise Men of the East when they came to worship a newborn baby in a manger at Bethlehem one long ago momentous night. Every king that had worn it since then had reigned well and uprightly, and had been loved by all his people; but only to the king was it known what virtue lay in this golden crown; and every king at dying gave it to his son and heir to the throne with the same words of blessing.

The king's eldest son wore the crown; and his step-mother knew that her own son could not wear the crown while he lived; therefore, she looked on and said nothing while her stepson was known to all the people of his country, because of his right to the throne, as the king's son; and his brother, the child of the second wife, was called the queen's son.

After the king's death, the queen was made regent until the king's son would be of full adult age and then able to manage the affairs of state; but already the little king wore the royal crown his father had left him, and the queen looked on and said nothing.

More than three years went by, and everybody said how good the queen was to the little king who was not her own son; and the king's son, for his part, was good to her and to his step-brother, loving them both; and all by himself he kept thinking, having his thoughts guarded and circled by his golden crown, "How shall I learn to be a wise king, and to be merciful when I have power?"

So to everything that came his way, to his playthings and his pets, to his ministers and his servants, he played the king as though already his word was like a sparkling pearl in an oyster. People watching him said, "Everyone that is touched by the king's son loves him." They told great tales of him. Only in fairy books could they be believed, because they were so beautiful; and all the time the queen, getting a good name for herself, looked on and said nothing.

TALES MY GRANDMOTHER TOLD ME

One night the king's son was lying half-asleep upon his bed, with wise dreams coming and going under the circle of his gold crown, when a mouse ran out of the small opening in a nearby wall and jumped up upon the couch. The poor mouse cried its news into the king's ear. "Oh king's son," it said, "get up and run for your life! I was behind the wall in the queen's closet, and I heard whispering that indicated if you stay here, you will not awaken in the morning, as there are plans to kill you."

Little did the king's son know that the mouse was actually an ally of the evil queen and arranged to be paid a vast amount of cheese to lure the king's son out of the palace, so that her villains could easily kill him outside in the nearby forest to avoid any suspicion the queen was involved.

The king's son got up and all alone in the dark night stole out of the palace, seeking safety for his dear life. He sighed to himself, "There was a pain in my crown ever since I wore it, for no one should ever be exalted as a king or queen. Alas, mother, I thought you were too kind a step-mother to do this, but I now see that the lure of my crown was why you were kind, because you wanted this crown, the wealth and the power for your son."

Outside it was still winter and there was no warmth in the world and not a leaf upon the trees. He wandered away, trying to decide where he should hide.

The queen, when the villains she had sent to kill the king's son came back to her quarters and told her the king's son was not to be found in the forest where they expected him to be, went and looked in her magic crystal ball to find a trace of him. As soon as it grew light, for in the darkness the crystal could show her nothing, she saw many kilometres away the king's son running to hide himself in the forest. So she sent out her villains to search until they could find him. As they went, the sun grew hot in the sky, and eventually they came upon a vast forest.

The king's son, stumbling along through the forest thought, "Even here, where shall I hide? Nowhere is there a leaf to cover me." But when the sun grew warm he looked up; and there were all the trees breaking into bud and leaf, making a green heaven above his head. So when he was too weary to go farther, he climbed into the largest tree he could find, and the leaves covered him.

The queen's villains searched through all the forest but could not find him. So they went back to her empty handed, not having either the king's crown or his heart to show. "Fools!" she cried, looking in her magic crystal, "he was in the big sycamore under which you stopped to give your horses a rest."

She looked in the crystal, but little could she see; for the king's son had hidden himself by then in a small cave on the side of a mountain where the crystal's eyes could not pierce.

Presently, she saw a flight of birds crossing the blue sky, and every bird carried a few crumbs of bread in its beak. Then she ran and called to her villains, "Follow the birds and they will take you to where he is; for they are carrying bread to feed

TALES MY GRANDMOTHER TOLD ME

him, and they are all heading for the mountain just outside the forest.

The birds said to the king's son, "Now you are rested and fed. The queen's eye is on you. Up, and run for your life!"

"Where shall I go?" asked the king's son. "Go," answered the birds, "and hide yourself in the marshes on the island of the pool of sweet waters! There, there are fish that will help you survive, for they are not poisoned with greed and envy."

When the queen's villains came to the mountain and found the cave, it was as though a thousand people had been feeding, because they found so many crumbs lying in the cave, but no king's son could they lay their hands on, because he was lying hidden among the tall reeds deep in the marches of a nearby island.

It took the queen three days of hard gazing in her crystal before she found how the fish all swam to a point among the reeds in the marshes of the island in the pool of sweet waters and away again. Then, she knew and running to her villains she cried, "He is among the reeds in the marshes on the island in the river near the mountain, and he is feeding on the tall reeds. Go, go, because the fish can feel my eyes gazing in the crystal and will warn him. Hurry, hurry!"

The fish, who had no greed or jealousy said to the king's son: "The queen's evil eye is on you, so swim to shore as quickly as possible and away for your life!"

"Where shall I go?" asked the king's son. "Wherever I go, she finds me."

J. WAYNE FRYE 49

"Go to the old fox who gets his poultry from the palace, and ask him to hide you in his burrow!"

When the queen's soldiers came to the pool they found the fish playing all about in the water, but nothing of the king's son could they see.

The king's son came to the fox, and the fox hid him in his burrow, and brought him butter and eggs from the royal dairy. This was better fare than the king's son had had since the beginning of his wanderings, and he thanked the fox warmly for his friendship.

The queen hugged her magic crystal for a whole week with the intention of finally finding the king's son, but could make nothing out of it, for her crystal could not discern the king's son's hiding-place, nor discover the fox at his nightly thefts of butter and eggs from the royal dairy. But it must be remembered that the fox is a wily creature, the kind of creature that first and foremost looks after his own welfare. Thus, the fox thought that if he revealed where the king's son was that he might curry favour with the queen; and thereby, get permanent access to the royal diary for his loyalty. It was then that he went to the queen to reveal where the king's son was hiding.

When the fox did not return at the expected time, the king's son grew suspicious and asked himself if he had not been betrayed? The queen had much to offer, and in a world that, like today, was based on greed and self-interest, the fox would, no doubt, bow before the altar of riches. The king's son knew that the foxes of the world were required to steal for survival, because the many were denied sustenance while the few gorged at the table of plenty. He had been one of the few who had power, but now he saw the folly of a world where the powerful would commit evil acts to maintain their exalted status. His stepmother had great wealth and power, but it was not enough, because those at the top are never satisfied. They must always have more and more. Thus is the evil of greed.

The queen had said to her villains, "Go and look in the fox's hole and you shall find him!" But the villains came and dug up the burrow, and found butter and eggs from the royal dairy, but of the king's son never a sign, because the king's son had determined that maybe the best place to hide was in plain sight, so he put on a disguise and crept through the palace gardens until he managed to go inside the palace through a secret entrance.

He hid in the dungeon below the castle, never parting with the crown, the very crown that the three wise men had brought to that newborn baby lying in a manger in Bethlehem. It was a crown that had never been worn by the one to whom it was first given, because that baby in the manger grew into a man who saw the folly of self-aggrandizement, and knew that a man or woman's worth should not be judged by the crown they wore, the clothes that adorned them, the house in which they lived or by the size of their wealth. He was a humble man who knew the content of one's character was the true measure of wealth. The king's son understood this.

The king's son spent many years hiding in the dungeon, where his brother, who became king in his absence, along with his mother, sent many of those who dared oppose them to be tortured and killed. He cowered in fear all those years, and would often put on that crown and stare out at the moat and long to be free, but he was afraid, afraid of death at the hands of the tyrants who ruled the land. One day though, as he stood wearing that crown, he reached up, took it off and tossed it into the water below. He grabbed a sword that had been left by one of the torturers and said to himself, "I am running no more. If they want to torture me, so be it. I have been in this dungeon, hiding in fear for years just to stay alive. Well, being afraid of your oppressors is not living. I am prepared now to die, because living on my knees before tyrants is no option. There is but one enemy of all the people, and that enemy is the rich and powerful who demand obedience."

He stormed out of that dungeon, up the stone stairs, and scurried down the hallway, where he slew guard after guard who challenged him. He felt no remorse at slaying them, because they had all bowed before tyrants so that they might live a privileged existence by ignoring the plight of the normal people. His fury rose and rose, as he stormed into the main hall where his evil half-brother and the cruel queen were on their thrones as they were being entertained by dancers. The guards rushed his way, but his mighty sword showed no mercy as he dispatched guard after guard.

TALES MY GRANDMOTHER TOLD ME

The king's son said to all left standing in awe at his fierceness, "You can all cower in fear. You can continue to bow before these prancing peacocks of royalty who got their positions of power by heredity and through the ruthless dispatching and suppression of all who opposed their tyranny, or you can stand with me, a man who does not want to be king, because no man should be so exalted as to be called king of anyone. There was a baby born in a manger long ago who was given a crown by three wise men, and that baby grew into a man who was exalted as king of all humanity, but he never wore a crown, never proclaimed himself a king. He had no fine clothes, no luxurious mansion, not even food unless it was given by those who loved him. Are you going to stay on your knees or are you going to demand justice and end tyranny?"

It is said that people actually line up for their chains, and on this day the king's son stood and waited as the poor souls actually stood there staring at their oppressors on their golden thrones, actually thinking about whether they wanted freedom or slavery? Thus, the king's son waited and waited for the oppressed to decide whether to get off their knees or not.

They all turned on him, and he had not the heart to slay the poor souls who had been so brainwashed that they were no longer capable of embracing freedom. They had rather live in slavery than throw off their shackles and think for themselves. They trampled him to death and turned to bow before their masters.

TALES MY GRANDMOTHER TOLD ME

<u>*Author's Comment*</u>

A few years after my grandmother's death, I recalled this tale, because I found it interesting that one of my heroes, Muhammad Ali, seemed to parrot my grandmother's story about the king's son.

"I ain't draft dodging. I ain't burning no flag. I ain't running to Canada. I'm staying right here. You want to send me to jail? Fine, you go right ahead. I've been in jail for 400 years. I could be there for four or five more, but I ain't going no 10,000 miles to help murder and kill other poor people. If I want to die, I'll die right here, right now, fightin' you, if I want to die. You my enemy, not no Chinese, no Vietcong, no Japanese. You my opposer when I want freedom. You my opposer when I want justice. You my opposer when I want equality. Want me to go somewhere and fight for you? You won't even stand up for me right here in America, for my rights and my religious beliefs. You won't even stand up for my rights here at home! ....Muhammad Ali

TALES MY GRANDMOTHER TOLD ME

Chapter 4
Rest in Each Others Arms for Eternity

Be leery of first impressions,
For abominations are sometimes
Defined by the abominable!

"This is a strange and terrible story my grandson, and though I am sixty-six years of age, I scarcely dare even now to disturb the ashes of that memory told me by my own mother. To you I can refuse nothing though, and you have asked for a story to tingle the spine; but I should not relate such a tale to any less experienced mind, for now you are a young man and can handle things, handle the macabre. You have an inquiring mind, and the two of us have shared many stories together, but this one I have never told you, because it is stranger than any fairy tale I ever shared in your youth. So strange were the circumstances of this story that I can scarcely believe what happened to my childhood friend and dear cousin, Daryl Hopkins. For a very long time he remained the victim of a most singular and diabolical illusion or delusion – you can decide. One single look too freely cast upon a woman well-nigh caused him to lose his soul, but finally he succeeded in casting out the real evil spirit that had possessed him. Or did he? Or was he confused about who the real devil was?"

"His daily life was long interwoven with a nocturnal life of a totally different character. By day he was a quiet, well-respected, a hard worker at the sawmill and on Sundays he was a minister at the nearby local church, but by night, from the instant that he closed his eyes he became a young nobleman, a fine connoisseur of women, dogs, and horses; gambling, drinking, and blaspheming; and when he awoke at early daybreak, it seemed to him, on the other hand, that he had been sleeping, and had only dreamed about a life of debauchery. Of this somnambulistic life there now remains only the faint recollection of certain scenes and words he shared so many years ago with my mother, which cannot be banished from memory. Although he never actually left the bedroom where his dreams seemed to be reality, he was a man who, weary of all worldly pleasures in those dreams, felt his sinfulness, even if only in dreams, would doom him to hell."

I sat enthralled by my dearly beloved grandmother's tale spinning artistry, as she related how Daryl Hopkins had once loved as none in the world ever loved, with an insensate and furious passion so violent that he was astonished it did not cause his heart to burst asunder. Ah, what nights he lived, nights that seared the soul. What nights!

From his earliest childhood he had felt a calling to the ministry, which is why he became the Sunday morning dispenser of hellfire and brimstone to those who want to be told how a vengeful God will rain down torrents of misery upon any who dare violate his will. Yet, Daryl was becoming a rarity in the ministry, because he found himself questioning the judgementalism of religion and began to feel rumblings deep within that rattled his adherence to an idea that some omnipotent all powerful creator up in the sky was controlling everyone's life. He began to feel he was blasphemous, that his dreams were destroying his devout nature.

He, even at 23, had never gone into the real world. His world was confined by the walls of the house he lived in with his parents, on a road called, of all things, New Hope Road, and his constant study of God's word. He knew in a vague sort of a way that there was something called a woman, but he never permitted his thoughts to dwell on such a subject, and he lived in a state of perfect innocence.

After awhile, he regretted nothing; he felt not the least hesitation at taking the last irrevocable step to sleep, because in sleep he was filled with joy and embraced the dreams that became his only joy in life. He was slowly becoming the victim of an inexplicable fascination.

He had been preaching at the local church since he was 16, but had never been formally ordained by the Baptist Church hierarchy, but one Sunday he was to be officially ordained by a church official coming all the way from the state Capitol in Raleigh, North Carolina. As the great day came, he walked to the church with a step so light that he fancied himself sustained in air with wings upon his shoulders. He believed himself to be an angel, and wondered at the sombre and thoughtful faces of his accompanying proud parents, for he felt they should be as buoyant as he was. That night he had not dreamed his usual dream of debauchery, but had passed all the night in prayer, and was in a condition bordering on ecstasy because of what was about to occur in church, and because he had not dreamed of the debauchery that usually filled his nights. Although he missed the dream in his heart, in his mind he felt that maybe they were finally over, and when he became an ordained minister they would be gone forever. In fact, the deacon sent to ordain him, a venerable old man, seemed to him to be God the Father leaning over his eternity. In his mind he beheld heaven through the flickering sun dancing about the stained glass in the church as he accidentally lifted his head, which until then he had kept down for the blessing being bestowed upon him, and beheld before him, so close that it seemed that he could have touched her, although she was actually a considerable distance from him and on the further side of the sanctuary railing, a young woman of extraordinary beauty, who was attired with royal magnificence. It seemed as though scales had suddenly fallen from his eyes. He felt like a blind man who unexpectedly recovers his sight. The deacon, so radiantly glorious but an instant before, suddenly vanished away, the tapers paled upon their golden candlesticks like stars in the dawn, and a vast darkness seemed to fill the whole church. The charming creature appeared in bright relief against the background of that darkness, like some angelic revelation. She seemed herself radiant, and radiating light rather than receiving it, as he lowered his eyelids, firmly resolved not to again open them, for fear he might be influenced by external objects, for distraction had gradually taken possession of him until he hardly knew what he was doing. Still, opening his eyes was not necessary in order to see her in all her luminous grandeur, because the vision of the incredible creature was indelibly burned like a hot branding iron into his mind. It was a brand that seared his brain, scorched it with a tenaciousness that was fanatical.

Oh, how beautiful she was! The greatest painters, who followed ideal beauty into heaven itself, and thence brought back to earth the true portrait of a woman's grandeur, never in their delineations even approached that wildly beautiful reality which he saw before him. Neither the verses of the poet nor the palette of the artist could convey any conception of her with any justice. She was rather tall, with a form and bearing of a goddess. Her hair, of a soft dark hue, was parted in the midst and flowed back over her temples in two rivers of rippling, shinning magnificence. She seemed a diademed queen. Her forehead extended its calm breadth above the arches of her eyebrows, which by a strange singularity were coal black, and admirably relieved the effect of dark brown eyes of unsustainable vivacity and brilliancy. What eyes! With a single flash they could have decided a man's destiny. They had a life, a limpidity, an ardour, a humid light which he had never seen in human eyes; they shot forth rays like arrows, which he could distinctly see enter his heart. He knew not if the fire which illumined them came from heaven or from hell, but assuredly it came from one or the other. That woman was either an angel or a demon, perhaps both.

Her teeth of the most lustrous pearl white gleamed in her ruddily brilliant smile, and at every inflection of her lips little dimples appeared in the satiny rose of her adorable cheeks. There was a delicacy and pride in the regal outline of her nostrils bespeaking noble blood. Agate gleams played over the smooth lustrous skin of her half-bare shoulders, and strings of pearls descended upon her generous bosom. From time to time she elevated her head with the undulating grace of a startled serpent or peacock; thereby, imparting a quivering motion to the high lace ruff which surrounded it like a mother hugging a newborn child.

She wore a robe of orange-red velvet, and from her wide ermine-lined sleeves there peeped forth patrician hands of infinite delicacy, and appeared so ideally transparent that they permitted the light to shine through them.

Through his mesmerized state he was greatly troubled at the time, but nothing escaped him; the faintest touch of shading, the little dark speck at the point of her chin, the imperceptible down at the corners of the lips, the velvety floss upon the brow and the quivering shadows of the eyelashes upon the cheek. He could notice everything with astonishing lucidity of perception.

He felt opening within him gates that had, until then remained closed. Vents so long obstructed became a crystal clear perception of certainty, permitting glimpses of unfamiliar perspectives within. Life suddenly made itself visible to him under a totally novel aspect.

He felt as though he had just been born into a new world and a new order of things. A frightful anguish commenced to torture his heart as with red-hot pincers. Every successive minute seemed to him at once but a second and yet a century. Meanwhile the ceremony was proceeding, and he shortly found himself transported far from that world of which his newly born desires were furiously besieging the entrance. Nevertheless, he answered "Yes" to the questions of fidelity to Biblical certainties put to him by the deacon when he wished to say "No," though all within him protested against the uncertainties done to his soul. Some occult power seemed to force the words from his throat against his will. Thus it is, perhaps, that so many young girls walk to the altar firmly resolved to refuse in a startling manner the husband imposed upon them, and that yet not one ever fulfils her intention; therefore, doubtless, many poor novices take the veil, though they have resolved to tear it into shreds at the moment when called upon to utter the vows. One dares not thus cause so great a scandal to all present, nor deceive the expectation of so many people. All those eyes, all those wills seem to weigh down like a cope of lead, and, moreover, measures have been so well taken, everything has been so thoroughly arranged beforehand and after a fashion so evidently irrevocable, that the will yields to the weight of circumstances and utterly breaks down. He wanted to forsake his vows, now with open eyes and run off into oblivion with the magnificent creature that was still imbedded deep within his mind, a mind that did not realize all that occurred was occurring in a fraction of a second, but seemed like an eternity.

As the ceremony proceeded, the features of the fair unknown woman changed their expression. Her look had at first been one of caressing tenderness; it changed to an air of disdain and of mortification at not having been able to make herself understood to Daryl. With an effort of will sufficient to have uprooted a mountain, Daryl Hopkins strove to cry out that he could not be a minister, but he could not speak; his tongue seemed nailed to his palate, and he found it impossible to express his will by the least syllable of negation. Though fully awake, he felt like one under the influence of a nightmare, who vainly strives to shriek out the one word upon which life depends. How could he be in the throes of a nightmare and of the most magnificent dream imaginable at the same time, a dream where the perfect woman stood in all her radiance before him?

The woman seemed conscious of the martyrdom he was undergoing, and, as though to encourage him, she gave him a look replete with divine promise. Her eyes were a poem; their every glance was a song. She said to him, "If thou wilt be mine, I shall make thee happier than God himself in his heavenly paradise. The angels themselves will be jealous of thee. Tear off that ridiculous minister's shroud in which thou art about to wrap thyself. I am beauty. I am youth. I am desire. I am life. I am hope. I am honesty unencumbered by judgemental arrogance. I am not bound by the hypocrisy of finger-pointers. Come to me! Together we shall embrace in ecstasy few can imagine. Can the Jehovah these people use to instil fear offer thee this much? Our lives will flow on like a dream, in one eternal kiss. Fling forth the wine of that chalice, and thou art free. I will conduct thee to delights you could never even imagine. Thou shalt sleep on my bosom upon a bed of massy gold under a silver pavilion, for I love thee and would take thee away from this cruel God who destroys rather than builds, before whom so many noble hearts pour forth floods of fake love which never reach even the steps of his throne! Come with me and be a slave to love."

These words seemed to float to his ears in a rhythm of infinite sweetness, for her look was actually sonorous, and the utterances of her eyes conveyed those words to the depths of his heart as though living lips had breathed them into his unconscious mind. He felt himself willing to renounce God, and yet his tongue mechanically fulfilled all the formalities of the ceremony. The fair woman gave him another look, so beseeching, so despairing that sharp, serrated blades seemed to pierce his heart. Then, like a symbol clanging the rousing crescendo of a symphony, he heard the words of the deacon, "It is done."

All was consummated; he was a minister by decree now. With those words, never was deeper anguish painted on human face than upon the beautiful apparition. She looked like the maiden who beholds her affianced lover suddenly fall dead at her side, the mother bending over the empty cradle of her child, the miser who finds a stone substituted for his treasure, the poet who accidentally permits the only manuscript of his finest work to fall into the fire.

No woman ever wore a look so despairing, so inconsolable. All the blood had abandoned her charming face, leaving it whiter than marble; her beautiful arms hung lifelessly on either side of her body as though their muscles had suddenly relaxed, and she sought the support of a pillar, as her yielding limbs almost betrayed her. Meanwhile, the newly ordained minister staggered toward the door of the church, livid as death, his forehead bathed with a sweat, because he felt like he was being strangled.

The entire congregation was in shock at his actions, and could not understand why he was staring at the nothingness before him. As he was about to cross the threshold to go outside for air, an invisible hand to all but him had suddenly caught his hand! It was cold as a serpent's skin, and yet its impress remained upon his wrist, burnt there as though branded by a glowing iron. In a sorrowful tone the apparition said, "Unhappy man! Unhappy man! What hast thou done?" Then she immediately disappeared into the crowd.

The aged deacon stood by his side in awe. He cast a severe and scrutinising look upon Daryl Hopkins, who seemed to be totally mesmerized by something that was not visible to anyone else. Daryl's face presented the absolute wildest aspect imaginable. He blushed and turned exceedingly pale alternately as dazzling lights flashed before his blinking eyes. A concerned parishioner took great pity on him, seized his arm and led him outside. The parishioner whispered, "It is O.K. It is all the excitement. It has simply overwhelmed you."

At the corner of a road, while Daryl's attention was momentarily turned in another direction, an unknown man, fantastically garbed in great finery, approached him, and without pausing on his way slipped into his hand a little pocket-book with gold-embroidered corners, while at the same time giving him a sign to hide it. Daryl concealed it in his breast coat pocket, and there kept it until he found himself alone back in the small room where he slept at his parent's home. Then he opened the clasp. There was only one page within, bearing the words, *Charlotte. At the Compton.*

So little acquainted was he at that time with the things of this world that he had never been to the elaborate Compton Gardens Hotel. He hazarded a thousand conjectures, each more extravagant than the last; but, in truth, he cared little for where he was supposed to meet the woman, as long as he could meet her, because he instinctively knew that she was the lady he had seen in the church. It was not an apparition, or if it was, then the real life woman had somehow projected herself into his presence in a mystical manner that made her visible to only him, and was now luring him to a genuine in the flesh meeting. Regardless, whether apparition or a real-live-in-the-flesh woman, he could not reject the opportunity to see her once more. He had lost all power to resist a woman that had imprinted his soul.

His love for this woman, although the growth of a few minutes at best, had taken imperishable root. That woman had completely taken possession of his mind. One look from her had sufficed to change his very nature. She had breathed her will into his life, and he no longer lived in himself, but in her and for her. He kissed the place upon which her handwriting was apparent. He repeated her name over and over again in relentless succession. He only needed to close his eyes in order to see her distinctly as though she were actually present; and he reiterated to himself the words she had uttered.

He comprehended at last the full horror of his situation, and the awful restraints of the state into which he had just entered became clearly revealed to him. He had lost his commitment to the ministry, because now all he cared about was wrapping this woman in his arms and doing her bidding, no matter how ungodly it might be. She had become his god.

He felt life rising within him like a subterranean lake, expanding and overflowing; his blood leaped fiercely through his arteries; his long-restrained youth suddenly burst into active being, like the aloe which blooms but once in a hundred years, and then bursts into blossom with a clap of thunder.

He walked by his mother and father without a word, walking outside as they sat dumbfounded by his apparent trance-like state, but they assumed it was just a result of all the excitement from the ordination. They decided to not press him, but rather, to let him wander away in the grips of deep thought.

The sky was beautifully blue; the trees had donned their spring robes; nature seemed to be making parade of an ironical joy. The town was filled with people, some going, others coming; young beaus and young beauties were sauntering in couples toward the groves and gardens; merry youths passed by, cheerily trolling refrains of songs. It was all a picture of vivacity, life, animation, gaiety, which formed a bitter contrast with his lingering desire to be in Charlotte's presence. On the steps of the park gate sat a young mother playing with her child. She kissed its little rosy mouth still impearled with drops of milk, and performed, in order to amuse it; a thousand divine little puerilities such as only mothers know how to invent. The father standing at a little distance smiled gently upon the charming two, and with folded arms seemed to hug joy to his heart. Daryl could not endure that spectacle of happiness, because he wanted that, too. He wanted to be with the woman who had captured his heart. He closed off all about him as he sat forlornly on a nearby bench.

While writhing on the bench in a fit of spasmodic emotional fury, he suddenly perceived the deacon, who was standing erect in front of him, watching attentively the young man who had just been ordained.

"Daryl, my dear young man, something very extraordinary is transpiring within you, as your conduct during and after the induction ceremony is altogether inexplicable. You are always so quiet, so pious, so gentle, but there is a rage within you growing like a wild beast! Take heed; do not listen to the suggestions of the devil, the evil spirit, furious that you have consecrated yourself forever to the Lord Jesus. That evil entity is prowling around you like a ravening wolf and making a last effort to obtain possession of you. Instead of allowing yourself to be conquered, make yourself a paragon of virtue, a buckler of mortifications, and combat the enemy like a valiant man; you will then assuredly overcome him. Virtue must be proved by temptation, and gold comes forth purer from the hands of the assayer. Fear not. Never allow yourself to become discouraged. The most watchful and steadfast souls are at moments liable to such temptation. Pray, fast, meditate and the evil spirit will depart from you."

Taking a deep breath, Daryl responded, "But is it wrong to be attracted to a woman, someone who appears to shine a light of hope that it seems I am unable to truly find in a religion that has taught me to judge others despite Jesus saying 'Judge not that ye not be judged?' She seems the embodiment of what religion should be. She seems angelic in the truest way. She appears to challenge so much of what I have been taught by the church."

TALES MY GRANDMOTHER TOLD ME

"I came not to banter about your doubts," the deacon offered, "but to tell you that you have been appointed as a minister for a church in Denton. Be ready to go with me tomorrow, so I can introduce you to the church elders and you can prepare for what you have been waiting for all your life."

He responded with an inclination of the head, and a long sigh. He said nothing as they walked back toward his parent's house. He may have said nothing but deep within he was talking to himself, saying that he could not leave without meeting Charlotte.

Then suddenly it recurred to him as he said goodbye to the deacon, the words of the artifices of the devil; and the strange character of the adventure, the supernatural beauty of Charlotte, the phosphoric light of her eyes, the burning imprint of her hand, the agony into which she had thrown him, the sudden change wrought within him when all piety vanished in a single instant. These and other things clearly testified to the work of the evil one he thought, and perhaps that satiny hand was but the glove which concealed her claws. He decided not to see her at the hotel.

Next morning, the deacon came to take him away. Two mules awaited the two at the gate. The deacon mounted one, and Daryl the other with trepidation, because he did not want to go.

As they passed along the streets of the city, he gazed attentively at all the windows and balconies in the hope of seeing Charlotte somewhere, anywhere, but it was early in the morning and the city had hardly opened its eyes. He sought to penetrate the blinds and window-curtains of all the places before which they were passing. Daryl had never even been to Denton as an adult, only as a very small child. They had journeyed for nearly three hours over hill and dell when the deacon noticed Daryl had gone into an almost trance-like state. They made it to the summit of a high hill when Daryl turned to take a long look at the valley to their right. He had never been this route before, and was frightened by the shadow of a great cloud that hung over them against the contrasting colours of the blue and red roofs below that were lost in a uniform half-tint, through which here and there floated upward, like white flakes of foam, the smoke of freshly kindled fires. By a singular optical effect, one edifice which surpassed in height all the neighbouring buildings that were still dimly veiled by the vapours, towered up, fair and lustrous with the gilding of a solitary beam of sunlight. Although actually more than a kilometre away, it seemed quite near. The smallest details of its architecture were plainly distinguishable, the turrets, the platforms, the window-casements, and even the swallow-tailed weather-vanes.

"What is that palace I see over there, all lit up by the sun?" Daryl asked the deacon.

The deacon shaded his eyes with his hand, and having looked in the direction indicated, replied: "There is nothing there my son. You are seeing an illusion. There was once a huge mansion outside the town, there to the right, but it was burned down, to destroy the abominations that dwelled there so long ago. There is no remnant of the place where once evil abided. You do not know that place my son? Many people do not, because it was long ago, and all blotted out the memories, as that was over 200 years ago, and all who were present are long dead, and the stories of what happened have died too, as they should, because that place was so evil, so horrible that even to remember it is also an abomination. When my great grandfather told me of it, he shuttered and shook, remembering the tale his grandfather had told him. It is the ancient place where the Prince of Darkness was conjured up from hell by witches and warlocks to marry the evil Angel of Abominations named Charlotte. Awful things were done there; awful, dreadful things that no one hereabouts has spoken of in woe so many years."

At that instant, Daryl, not knowing whether it was reality or an illusion, fancied he saw gliding along the terrace of the stately place below in the distance a shapely white figure, which gleamed for a moment in passing and as quickly vanished. It was Charlotte. It had to be, but why could not the deacon see the place. Why was it only visible to Daryl?

Oh, did Charlotte know that at that very hour, all feverish and restless from the height of the rugged road which separated him from her, Daryl's eyes and passion were concentrated upon the mansion where she dwelt, as a mocking beam of sunlight seemed to bring to him an invitation to enter therein as its lord, as her mate to replace the Prince of Darkness whom she now had apparently deserted, or who had deserted her. Undoubtedly she must have known of Daryl's presence, for her soul was too sympathetically united with his not to have felt its least emotional thrill, and that subtle sympathy it must have been which prompted her to climb, although clad only in her nightdress to the summit of the terrace, amid the icy dews of the morning in that illusionary mansion that was playing a symphony of desire in Daryl's head.

The shadow gained the palace, and the scene became to his eye only a motionless ocean of roofs and gables, amid which one mountainous undulation was distinctly visible. The deacon urged his mule forward, as he grabbed the reins of Daryl's mule, forcefully pulling him away while saying, "Turn your eyes from that place where evil dwells. I know not what you are thinking or seeing, but believe me that place is evil. Put it from your mind."

Daryl felt an urge to grab the reins from the deacon, turn his mule and gallop to that place, gallop into the arms of Charlotte, but he had no energy, no ability to flee from what awaited him just over the hill in Denton, as the morning came into full bloom, and he saw the steeple of the church which he was to take charge of, peeping above the trees.

Following the downhill descent of the winding road fringed with cottages and little gardens, the two men found themselves in front of the façade of the ornate church, which certainly possessed many features of magnificence in an otherwise blighted area. The parsonage was small but splendorous, containing a porch ornamented with some mouldings, and three pillars hewn from sandstone; an elaborately tiled roof, and a gold embossed door. To the left lay the cemetery, overgrown with high weeds, and having a great iron cross rising up in its centre. Both stood to the right in the dark, almost sinister shadow of the church.

They walked into the house of extreme, almost austere, cleanliness that was filled with expensive furnishings that made Daryl think how any man of God could live in such luxury while the parishioners had to struggle day-to-day and many obviously lived in poverty as evidenced by what he saw entering the town.

A very old woman, Celeste, who was the housekeeper, came forward to greet them, and after having invited the two into a little back parlour, asked whether Daryl intended to retain her. He replied that he would take care of her, and the dog that came into the parlour. At this she became fairly transported with joy.

Thereupon, the deacon departed, wishing Daryl good luck and encouraging him to get in touch if he needed anything. He was; therefore, left alone, with the old woman who quickly retired to her quarters in the back of the house.

Daryl sat in the parlour thinking of Charlotte. The thought of Charlotte and that vision of her he saw just over the hill from Denton again began to haunt him, and in spite of all his endeavours to banish it, he always found it present in his meditations. One evening, while promenading in the little garden bordering the house, he fancied that he saw through the elm-trees the figure of a woman, who followed his every movement, and that he beheld two sea-green eyes gleaming through the foliage; but it was only an illusion, and upon going around to the other side of the garden, he could find nothing except a footprint on the sanded walkway, a footprint so small that it seemed to have been made by a child. "Could ghosts make footprints?" he asked himself.

The garden was enclosed by very high walls. He searched every nook and corner of it, but could discover no one there. He could never succeed in fully accounting for this circumstance, which, after all, was nothing compared with the strange things which happened to him afterward.

For a whole year he lived thus, filling all the duties of his calling with the most scrupulous exactitude, praying and fasting, exhorting and lending generous aid to the sick, and bestowing alms even to the extent of frequently depriving himself of the very necessaries of life, because he felt abominably to live in luxury as he did while most of the parishioners lived either in poverty or on the edge of poverty. Of course, the few well-off parishioners had their separate pews at the front of the church so they could be separated from the riff-raff, because even religion in a society where greed ruled supreme had to give privilege to the moneyed class.

Daryl had never accepted the hypocrisy of religion. He abhorred the finger-pointing and the accusatory nature of those who wanted to impose a rigid set of rules divined by those with a holier-than-thou attitude. Oh, but now he was face-to-face with the reality of a world where the economic divisions were excused with the "God will take care of you attitude" that insisted people accept their fate and not stand against the authority of the church and government. He felt a great aridness within, and the sources of grace seemed closed against him, because he was now questioning things that he had never questioned before.

He was unable to find any happiness which should spring from the fulfilment of a holy mission; his thoughts were far away, and the words of Charlotte that day were ever upon his lips like an involuntary refrain. Through having but twice lifted his eyes upon Charlotte, through one fault apparently so venial, he remained a victim to the most miserable agonies, and the happiness of his life had been destroyed forever by the memory of her.

One night his door knocker was long and violently pounded. The aged housekeeper arose and opened the door to the stranger, and the figure of a man, whose complexion was deeply bronzed, and who was richly clad in a foreign costume, appeared in the doorway. Her first impulse was one of terror, but the stranger reassured her, and stated that he desired to see the minister at once on matters relating to his holy calling. He was invited in and ushered into the parlour, where Daryl sat reading the Bible. The stranger told him that his mistress, a very noble lady, was lying at the point of death, and desired to see a minister. He replied that he was prepared to follow him, took with him the sacred articles necessary and left in all haste.

Two horses black as the night itself stood without the gate, pawing the ground with impatience, and veiling their chests with long streams of smoky vapour exhaled from their nostrils. The man held the stirrup and aided Daryl to mount upon one; then, merely laying his hand upon the pommel of the saddle, he vaulted on the other, pressed the animal's sides with his knees, and loosened rein. The horse bounded forward with the velocity of an arrow. Daryl's, of which the stranger held the bridle, also started off at a swift gallop, keeping up with his companion, as they seemed to figuratively devour the road. The ground flowed backward beneath them in a long streaked line of pale grey, and the black silhouettes of the trees seemed fleeing by them on either side like an army in a military rout of an enemy. They passed through a forest so profoundly gloomy that Daryl felt his flesh creep in the chilled darkness with superstitious fear. The showers of bright sparks which flew from the stony road under the iron-shod feet of the horses remained glowing in the wake like a fiery trail, and had any one at that hour of the night beheld them both they would have assumed them to be two spectres riding upon nightmares. Witchy fires and anon seemed to flitt across the road before them, and the night-birds shrieked fearsomely in the depth of the woods beyond, where they beheld at intervals, glowing phosphorescent eyes of wild animals. The manes of the horses became more and more dishevelled, the sweat streamed over their flanks, and their breath came through their nostrils hard and fast. But when Daryl's guide found them slacking pace, he reanimated them by uttering a strange, guttural, unearthly cry, and the gallop recommenced with fury. At last the whirlwind race ceased; a huge black mass pierced through with many bright points of light suddenly rose before them, the hoofs of the horses echoed louder upon a strong wooden drawbridge, and they rode under a great vaulted archway which darkly yawned between two enormous towers. Some great excitement evidently reigned in the mansion, as Daryl realized he knew the place. Yes, it was the place he had seen from the hilltop - the place where he had seen Charlotte.

Servants with torches were crossing the courtyard in every direction, and above lights were ascending and descending from landing to landing. He obtained a confused glimpse of vast masses of architecture – columns, arcades, flights of steps, stairways – a royal voluptuousness and elfin magnificence of construction worthy of a fairyland. A page, the same who had before brought him the tablet note from Charlotte in the churchyard, and whom he instantly recognised, approached to aid him in dismounting, and another obvious servant, attired in black velvet with a gold chain about his neck, advanced to meet Daryl, supporting himself upon an ivory cane. Large tears were falling from his eyes and streaming over his cheeks and white beard. "Too late!" he cried, sorrowfully shaking his venerable head. "Too late, sir! But if you have not been able to save the soul, come at least to watch by the poor body."

He took his arm and conducted him to the death-chamber. Daryl wept not less bitterly than the servant, for he looked down upon the body and realized it was none other than Charlotte, whom he had so deeply and so wildly loved from afar, with all his body and soul. In a chiselled urn upon the table there was a faded white rose, whose leaves, excepting one that still held, had all fallen, like odorous tears, to the foot of the vase. A broken black mask, a fan, and disguises of every variety, which were lying on the armchairs, bore witness that death had entered suddenly and unannounced into that sumptuous dwelling. Without daring to cast his eyes upon the bed, he knelt down and commenced to repeat the Psalms for the Dead, with exceeding fervour, thanking God that he had placed the tomb between him and the memory of this woman, so that he might thereafter be able to utter her name in prayers as a name forever sanctified by death. But his fervour gradually weakened, and he fell insensibly into a daydream. That chamber bore no semblance to a chamber of death. In lieu of the fetid and cadaverous odours which he had been accustomed to breathe during such funereal vigils, a languorous vapour of oriental perfume softly floated through the tepid air. That pale light seemed rather a twilight gloom contrived for voluptuous pleasure, than a substitute for the yellow-flickering watch-tapers which shine by the side of corpses. He thought upon the strange destiny which enabled him to meet Charlotte again at the very moment when she was lost to him forever, and a sigh of regretful anguish escaped from his breast. Then it seemed to him that some one behind him had also sighed, and he turned round to look. It was only an echo. But in that moment his eyes fell upon the bed of death which they had till then avoided. The red curtains, decorated with large flowers worked in embroidery and looped up with gold bullion, permitted him to behold the fair dead, lying at full length, with hands joined upon her bosom. She was covered with a linen wrapping of dazzling whiteness, which formed a strong contrast with the gloomy purple of the hangings, and was of so fine a texture that it concealed nothing of her body's charming form, and allowed the eye to follow those beautiful outlines, undulating like the neck of a swan, which even death had not robbed of their supple grace. She seemed an alabaster statue executed by some skilful sculptor to place upon the tomb of a queen, or rather, perhaps, like a slumbering maiden over whom the silent snow had woven a spotless veil.

He could no longer maintain his constrained attitude. The air of the alcove intoxicated him, that febrile perfume of half-faded roses penetrated his brain, and he commenced to pace restlessly up and down the chamber, pausing at each turn to contemplate the graceful corpse lying beneath the transparency of its shroud. Wild fancies came thronging to his brain. He thought to himself that she might not, perhaps, be really dead; that she might only have feigned death for the purpose of bringing him to her castle, and then declaring her love. At one time he even thought he saw her foot move under the whiteness of the coverings, and slightly disarrange the long straight folds of the winding-sheet.

And then he asked himself: "Is this indeed Charlotte? What proof is there it is she? Might not that person who gave him the note have passed into the service of some other lady?" But his heart answered with a fierce throbbing: "It is she; it is she indeed!"

He approached the bed again, and fixed his eyes with redoubled attention upon the object of his incertitude. That exquisite perfection of bodily form, although purified and made sacred by the shadow of death, affected him more voluptuously than it should have done; and that repose so closely resembled slumber that one might well have mistaken it for such. He forgot that he had come there to perform a funeral ceremony. He fancied himself a young bridegroom entering the chamber of the bride, who, with modestly, hides her fair face, and through coyness seeks to keep herself wholly veiled. Heartbroken with grief, yet wild with hope, shuddering at once with fear and pleasure, he bent over her and grasped the corner of the sheet. He lifted it back, holding his breath all the while through fear of waking her. His arteries throbbed with such violence that he felt them hiss through his temples, and the sweat poured from his forehead in streams, as though he had lifted a mighty slab of marble. There, indeed, lay Charlotte, as he had seen her as an illusion at the church on the day of his ordination. She was not less charming than then. With her, death seemed but another glorification of her beauty. The pallor of her cheeks, the less brilliant carnation of her lips, her long eyelashes lowered and relieving their dark fringe against that white skin, lent her an unspeakably seductive aspect of sensual beauty, but within that there was a look that seemed to project suffering. Her long loose hair, still intertwined with some little blue flowers, made a shining pillow for her head, and veiled the nudity of her shoulders with its thick ringlets; her beautiful hands were crossed on her bosom in an attitude of sensuousness, which served to make one realize that even in death she was alluring.

He remained long in mute contemplation, and the more he gazed, the less could he persuade himself that life had really abandoned that beautiful body forever. He did not know whether it was an illusion or a reflection of the lamplight, but it seemed to him that the blood was again commencing to circulate under that lifeless pallor, although she remained all motionless. He laid his hand lightly on her arm; it was cold, but not colder than her hand on the day when it touched his at the portals of the church. He resumed a position, bending his face above her, and bathing her cheek with the warm dew of his tears. Ah, what bitter feelings of despair and helplessness. What agonies unutterable did he endure in that long watch! Vainly did he wish that he could have gathered all his life into one mass that he might give it all to her, and breathe into her chill the flame which devoured him. The night inevitably advanced, and feeling the moment of eternal separation approach, he could not deny himself the last sad sweet pleasure of imprinting a kiss upon the dead lips of her who had been his only love, even though so brief, he knew he would never find such a love again.

Oh, miracle! A faint breath mingled itself with his breath, and the mouth of Charlotte responded to the passionate pressure of his lips. Her eyes unclosed, and lighted up with something of their former brilliancy. She uttered a long sigh, and uncrossing her arms, passed them around his neck with a look of ineffable delight. "Ah, it is thou, Daryl!" she murmured in a voice languishingly sweet as the last vibrations of a harp. "What ailed thee, dearest? I waited so long for thee that I am dead; but we are now betrothed: I can see thee and visit thee. Adieu, Daryl, adieu! I love thee. That is all I wished to tell thee, and I give thee back the life which thy kiss for a moment recalled. We shall soon meet again."

Her head fell back, but her arms yet encircled him, as though to retain him still. A furious whirlwind suddenly burst in though the open window, and entered the chamber. The last remaining leaf of the white rose for a moment palpitated at the extremity of the stalk like a butterfly's wing, and then it detached itself and flew forth through the open window, bearing with it the delightful soul of Charlotte. The lamp was extinguished, and Daryl fell insensible upon the bosom of the beautiful dead woman.

When he came to again he was lying on the bed in the ornate bedroom at his home, and Celeste who was trembling with age and anxiety, was busying herself about the room, opening and shutting drawers. On seeing Daryl open his eyes, the old woman uttered a cry of joy, but he was so weak that he could not speak a single word or make the slightest motion. Afterward, he learned that he had lain thus for three days, giving no evidence of life beyond the faintest respiration. Those three days did not reckon in his life, nor could he ever imagine whether his spirit had departed during those three days. Celeste told him that the same coppery-complexioned man who came to seek him on the night of his departure from the presbytery had brought him back the next morning in a near comatose state, and departed immediately afterward.

When he became able to collect his scattered thoughts, he reviewed within his mind all the circumstances of that fateful night. At first he thought he had been the victim of some magical illusion, but the long, tedious recollection of other circumstances, real and palpable in themselves, came to forbid that supposition. He could not believe that he had been dreaming, since Celeste as well as he had seen the strange man with his two black horses, and described with exactness every single detail of his figure and apparel. Nevertheless, it appeared that none knew of any palace-like mansion anywhere thereabouts in the area answering to the description of that in which he had again found Charlotte.

One morning Daryl found the deacon in his room, as Celeste had advised him that Daryl was ill, and he had come with all speed to see him. Although this haste on his part testified to an interest, maybe even affection for Daryl, his visit did not cause any pleasure which it should have done. The deacon had something penetrating and inquisitorial in his gaze, which made Daryl feel very ill at ease. His presence filled him with embarrassment and a sense of guilt. At the first glance he divined his interior trouble, and Daryl detested his clairvoyance.

While the deacon inquired after Daryl's health in hypocritically honeyed accents, he constantly kept his two great yellow lion-eyes fixed upon him. Then he asked how Daryl was doing directing the parish, if he was happy in it, how he passed the leisure hours and whether he had become acquainted with many of the inhabitants of the place, what was his favourite reading, and a thousand other such questions. He answered these inquiries as briefly as possible, and the deacon, without ever waiting for answers, passed rapidly from one subject of query to another. That conversation had evidently no connection with what he actually wished to say. At last, without any premonition, but as though repeating a piece of news which he had recalled on the instant, and feared might otherwise be forgotten subsequently, he suddenly said, in a clear vibrant voice, which rang in Daryl's ears like the trumpets of the Last

Judgment: "I understand that you took a ride in the dark of the night a while ago."

Daryl knew not how he found out, but decided that he might as well admit to it. Very tepidly he said, "I thought it to be a dream, but Celeste saw the horseman and the steeds that spirited me away, also."

He then recounted verbatim what had occurred. After listening intently, the deacon said, "The great courtesan Charlotte died long ago, at the close of an orgy which lasted eight days and eight nights. It was something infernally diabolical. The abominations of the banquets of Belshazzar and Cleopatra were re-enacted there. The guests were served by swarthy slaves who spoke an unknown tongue, and who seemed to be veritable demons. There have always been very strange stories told of this woman Charlotte and all her lovers came to a violent or miserable end. They used to say that she was a ghoul, a female vampire; but I believe she was none other than the bride of Beelzebub himself."

He ceased to speak, and commenced to regard Daryl more attentively than ever, as though to observe the effect of his words on him. This news of her long ago death, in addition to the pain it caused him by reason of its coincidence with the nocturnal scenes he had witnessed, filled him with an agony and terror which his face betrayed, despite his utmost endeavours to appear composed.

The deacon fixed an anxious and severe look upon him, and then observed: "My son, I must warn you that you are standing with foot raised upon the brink of an abyss; take heed lest you fall therein. Satan's claws are long, and tombs are not always true to their trust. The tomb of Charlotte should be sealed down with a triple seal, for, if report be true, it is not the first time she has died and then come mysteriously back to life in a re-manifested mansion below that hill where you apparently saw her on our way here. Be careful, because the devil is at play there." And with those words the deacon rose, turned and walked slowly out the door.

Daryl became completely restored to health and resumed his accustomed duties. The memory of Charlotte and the words of the deacon were constantly on his affected mind; nevertheless, no extraordinary event had occurred to verify the predictions of doom promulgated by the deacon, and Daryl had commenced to believe that the fears and terrors were over-exaggerated, when one night he had a strange dream. He had hardly fallen asleep when he heard a strange noise at the foot of the bed. He rose up quickly upon his elbow, and beheld the shadow of a woman standing erect before him. He recognized Charlotte immediately. She bore in her hand a little lamp, shaped like those which are placed in tombs, and its light lent her fingers a rosy transparency, which extended itself by lessening degrees even to the opaque and milky whiteness of her bare arm. Her only garment was the linen winding-sheet which had shrouded her when lying upon the bed of death. She sought to gather its folds over her bosom as though ashamed of being so scantily clad, but her little hand was not equal to the task. She was so white that the colour of the drapery blended with that of her flesh under the pallid rays of the lamp. Enveloped with this subtle tissue which betrayed all the contour of her body, she seemed rather the marble statue of some fair antique bather than a woman endowed with life. But dead or living, statue or woman, shadow or body, her beauty was still the same, only that the green light of her eyes was less brilliant, and her mouth, once so warmly crimson, was only tinted with a faint tender rosiness, like that of her cheeks. Nothing prevented her from being charming, so charming that, notwithstanding the strange character of the adventure, and the unexplainable manner in which she had entered Daryl's room, he felt not even for a moment the least bit of fear.

She gracefully moved to his bedside, placed the lamp on the table and seated herself at the foot of side of his bed; then bending toward him, she said, in that voice at once silvery clear and yet velvety in its sweet softness, such as he had never heard from any lips save hers: "I have kept thee long in waiting, dear Daryl, and it must have seemed to thee that I had forgotten thee. But I come from far off, very far off, and from a land whence few has ever yet returned. There is neither sun nor moon in that land from whence I come: all is but space and shadow; there is neither road nor pathway: no earth for the foot, no air for the wing; and nevertheless behold me here, for love is stronger than death and must conquer all in the end. Oh what sad faces and fearful things I have seen on my way hither! What difficulty my soul, returned to earth through the power of will alone, has had in finding its body and reinstating itself therein! What terrible efforts I had to make ere I could lift the ponderous slab with which they had covered me! See, the palms of my poor hands are all bruised! Kiss them, sweet love, that they may be healed!"

She laid the cold palms of her hands upon his lips, one after the other. He kissed them, indeed, many times, and she all the while watched him with a smile of ineffable affection.

Daryl had entirely forgotten the advice of the deacon and the sacred office wherewith he had been invested and ordained. He had fallen without resistance. He had not even made the least effort to repel the tempter. The fresh coolness of Charlotte's skin penetrated his own, and he felt arousing tremors pass over his whole body. He simply could not believe such a lovely creature could be a demon; at least she had no appearance of being such, and if she was, never did Satan so skilfully conceal his claws and horns. She had drawn her feet up beneath her, and squatted down on the edge of the chair by the bedside in an attitude of full sensualness. From time to time she passed her little hand through her hair and twisted it into curls, as though trying out how a new style of wearing it would be more enticing to Daryl. He abandoned himself to her hands with the guiltiest pleasure, while she accompanied her gentle play with the prettiest prattle. The most remarkable fact was that he felt no astonishment whatever at so extraordinary an adventure, and as in dreams one finds no difficulty in accepting the most fantastic events as simple facts, so all these circumstances seemed to me perfectly natural in themselves. He was absolutely the most enamoured of men. He was her captive in mind, body and spirit.

Still playing with her hair, her eyes bore into his with intense carnality as she said, "Thou loved me in your dreams, and in your nightly illusions of debauchery I could hear you calling for me, calling for a woman who could fulfill all your desires of not only the flesh but of the soul. Oh, but suddenly there you were in the church being ordained. Yet, I could feel you calling me, calling for me to save you from the hypocrisy of the cloth. I first saw thee in the flesh at the church at that fatal moment. I said at once, 'It is he who has called me in his dreams and now he wants me to save him from this fate!' I gave thee a look into which I threw all the love I ever had, all the love I now have, all the love I shall ever have for thee, a look that would have damned a cardinal or brought a king to his knees at my feet in view of all his court. Thou remained unmoved, preferring thy God of vengeance to me! Oh, how my heart ached. How my eyes filled with moisture at the loss of my love. Ah, how jealous I am of that God whom thou didst love and still love more than me! I writhed in misery in my darkened tomb to know that you have given your love to the church rather than me. Can you not see that the God they promote is used to point fingers of condemnation rather than love? Be not swayed by those who want to control your mind, control free thought."

She then looked upon him with sadness deep within her dark eyes, and said, "Woe is me, unhappy one that I am! I can never have thy heart all to myself. I, whom thou didst recall to life with a kiss upon my dead lips, longs for thee. It is for thee that I burst asunder the gates of the tomb, so that I could be transported to my bed, and lie in wait for your kiss to breathe life into me again. I desire real life with you rather than the illusionary life of your dreams."

All her words were accompanied with the most impassioned caresses, which bewildered Daryl's sense and reason to such an extent that he did not fear to utter a frightful blasphemy for the sake of consoling her, and to declare that he loved her as much as the God he had pledged allegiance to in that church.

Her eyes rekindled and shone like bright stars filling the firmament of heaven, bringing grand light to the darkness. The light of eternity shone from them, and locked within Daryl's heart the essence of love as he had never known before.

She flung her arms around him and said, "You love me more than that God you pledged allegiance to. Since it is so, come with me, follow me whithersoever I desire. Thou wilt cast away the ugliness of a church that teaches you to judge others, a church that lets the poor starve while it caters to the rich, a church that tells you about a reward in the end while you must suffer through life, a church that practices hypocrisy at ever avenue. Thou shalt be the proudest and most envied of cavaliers; thou shalt be my lover! To be the acknowledged lover of Charlotte, who has refused even a Pope long ago who wanted to share my bed! That will be something to feel proud of. Ah, the fair, unspeakably happy existence, the beautiful golden life we shall live together! And when shall we depart, my fair sir? Tell me when we shall start a life of blissful delirium."

"Tomorrow! Tomorrow! Tomorrow after I take care of preparations to join you in a life of which I have dreamed for so long," Daryl cried in rapturous delight.

"Tomorrow, then, so let it be!" she answered. "In the meanwhile, I shall have opportunity to morph into a truly human form rather than the will-o'-the-wisp I am now. I must also forthwith notify all who serve me, so they can arrange money, the dresses, the carriages – all will be ready for us in the fairytale land that awaits us. I shall call for thee at this same hour. Adieu, dear heart!" And she lightly touched his forehead with her lips. The lamp went out, and all became dark. A leaden, dreamless sleep fell on him and held him unconscious until the morning following, when he woke to greet a day that he had longed for, a day that he had pursued for so long, a day when he would truly know the love of a grand woman.

He awoke later than usual, and the recollection of this singular adventure troubled him during the whole day. He finally persuaded himself that it was a mere vapour of his heated imagination.

Nevertheless its sensations had been so vivid that it was difficult to persuade himself that they were not real, and it was not without some presentiment of what was going to happen that he crawled into bed at last, after having prayed God to drive far from him all thoughts of evil, to protect the chastity of his slumber and to not tempt him with dreams of Charlotte.

He soon fell into a deep sleep, and his dream was continued. Then, he beheld Charlotte, not as on the former occasion, pale in her winding-shroud, with the violets of death upon her cheeks, but gay, sprightly, jaunty, in a superb travelling-dress of green velvet, trimmed with gold lace, and looped up on either side to allow a glimpse of satin smooth, alluring skin. Her blond hair escaped in thick ringlets from beneath a broad black felt hat, decorated with white feathers whimsically twisted into various shapes. In her right hand she held a little riding-crop. She tapped him lightly with it, and exclaimed: "Well, my fine sleeper, is this the way you make your preparations? I thought I would find you up and dressed. Arise quickly; we have no time to lose." She then got a mischievous smile upon her lips that curled devilishly to one side, as she whispered, "Maybe I should swat you a time or two to motivate you." Then her eyes twinkled with impishness as she continued, "I bet you'd like that."

He leaped out of bed at once, standing there in shock before her in his nightclothes, as she said, "Come, dress yourself, and let us go," as she continued, pointing to a little package she had brought with her. "The horses are becoming impatient of delay and champing their bits at the door. We ought to have been by this time at least ten leagues distant from here."

Almost catatonic, he dressed himself hurriedly, with the clothes from the now opened package Charlotte had brought, as she handed him the articles of apparel herself one by one, bursting into laughter from time to time at his awkwardness dressing himself before her. She hurriedly arranged his hair, and this done, moved seductively to him and said, "I am to have such a handsome and desirable lover!"

He was no longer the same person. He could not even recognise himself. He resembled his former self no more than a finished statue resembles a block of stone. His old face seemed but a coarse daub of the one reflected in the mirror that he was now gazing into. He was debonairly handsome, and his arrogant vanity was sensibly tickled by the metamorphosis. He was a dandy indeed!

He wondered from where the elegant apparel he was wearing had come. He had never seen any of it before. It made of him a totally different personage, and he marvelled at the power of transformation owned by a few yards of cloth cut after a certain pattern. The spirit of his costume penetrated his very skin and there was now an effervescing glow to it. He was alive, alive for the first time in his life. He had been dead, but now he had arisen from the tomb of life into another plain of existence where he was all he had dreamed of being.

In order to feel more at ease in his new attire, he took several turns up and down the room. Charlotte watched him with an air of maternal pleasure, and appeared well satisfied with her work. Smiling, she said, "Come, enough of this child's play! Let us start. We have far to go, and we may not get there in time."

She took his hand and led him forth. All the doors opened before her as if she was some type of wizard, and they passed though the final door out into the crisp night air where the same man who had whisked him away that faithful night waited, holding the bridles of three horses, all black like those which bore him before. They were as fleet as the wind itself, and the moon, which had just risen at their departure, lit the way as they rolled over the sky like chariot wheels pounding the arena in ancient Rome.

Soon they came upon a level plain where, hard by a clump of trees, a carriage with four vigorous coal-black horses awaited. They entered it, and immediately the animals were away in a mad gallop, despite their being no coachman to whip them into a frenzy. Daryl, with pounding heart and searing mind, put one arm around Charlotte's waist, and one of her hands clasped his; her head leaned upon his shoulder, and he felt her bosom, half bare, lightly pressing against his arm. He had never known such intense happiness. In that hour he had forgotten everything, and he no more remembered having ever been a minister than he remembered what he had been doing in his mother's womb, so great was the fascination which Charlotte's spirit exerted upon him. From that night his nature seemed in some sort to have become halved, and there were two men within him, neither of whom knew the other. At one moment he believed himself a minister who dreamed nightly that he was a dandy; at another that he was a gentleman who dreamed he was a minister. He could no longer distinguish the dream from the reality, nor could he discover where the reality began or where ended the dream. The exquisite young lord and libertine railed at the minister, the minister loathed the dissolute habits of the young lord. Two spirals entangled and confounded the one with the other. Only there was one absurd fact he could not explain, namely, that the consciousness of the same individuality existed in two men so opposite in character.

He fought within his mind to decide whether what was happening was illusion or reality. He found himself in a great palace filled with frescoes and statues that adorned every room. It was a palace well worthy of a king. It must have been in Venice, because they had a gondola where, as the dark faceless figure at the helm moved it effortlessly through the city, he and Charlotte made love in the black shrouded enclosure where they lay rapturously in each other's arms. They lived on a magnificent scale. There was something of Cleopatra in her nature, because she was more than queen, she was a temptress. As for Daryl, he had the retinue of a king, and I was regarded with as much reverential respect as though he had been from the family of one of the twelve Apostles which he had once, in what now seemed long ago, held in so much reverence.

Daryl revelled in what was once sin to him. Despite living as a nobleman, he found great pleasure in mingling with classes considered beneath his station in life. The poor beggars, the women of the street, those considered the dregs of society were embraced by him and by Charlotte. Through it all, he loved Charlotte wildly. To have Charlotte was to have twenty mistresses; to possess all women: so mobile, so varied of aspect, so fresh in new charms was she all in herself – a very chameleon of a woman who could be a wanton paramour, but have a heart that embraced those who had been tossed away by society, a society where worth was judged by money rather than character. He had assumed her sinful, but was the church just as sinful by bowing to the greed that afflicted mankind? How, he reflected, could the church build great edifices to the glory of God, when the real glory of God could be found not in the ostentatiously ornate churches, but in the simplicity of the poor who needed a hand up rather than a collection plate shoved in their faces? In this woman, he had found himself, found not the evil that he had been warned of, but a love returned a hundred-fold. Of gold she had enough. She wished no longer for anything but love, a love so pure angels would have cried with envy.

Reassured by his constant association with her, he never thought further of the strange manner in which he had become acquainted with Charlotte. But the words of the deacon concerning her recurred often to his memory, and never ceased to cause uneasiness.

For some time, the health of Charlotte had not been so good as usual; her complexion grew paler day by day. The physicians who were summoned could not comprehend the nature of her malady and knew not how to treat it. They all prescribed some insignificant remedies, and never called a second time. Her paleness, nevertheless, visibly increased, and she became colder and colder, until she seemed almost as white and dead as upon that memorable night in the unknown place. He grieved with anguish unspeakable to behold her thus slowly perishing; and she, touched by his agony, smiled upon him sweetly and sadly with the fateful smile of those who feel that they must die.

One morning Daryl was seated at her bedside, and breakfasting from a little table placed close at hand, so that he might not be obliged to leave her for a single instant. In the act of cutting some fruit he accidentally inflicted rather a deep gash on his finger. The blood immediately gushed forth in a little purple jet, and a few drops spurted upon Charlotte. Her eyes flashed, her face suddenly assumed an expression of savage and ferocious joy such as he had never before observed in her. She leaped out of her bed with animal agility, the agility, as it were, of an ape or a cat and sprang upon his wound, which she commenced to suck with an air of unutterable pleasure. She swallowed the blood in little mouthfuls, slowly and carefully, like a connoisseur tasting a wine. Gradually her eyelids half closed, and the pupils of her eyes became oblong instead of round. From time to time she paused in order to kiss his hand, and then she would recommence to press her lips to the wound in order to coax forth a few more ruddy drops. When she found that the blood would no longer easily spurt forth, she arose with eyes liquid and brilliant, rosier than a May dawn; her face full and fresh, her hand warm and moist, more beautiful than ever, and in the most perfect health. Her apparent happiness had been rejuvenated.

"I shall not die! I shall not die!" she cried, clinging to Daryl's neck, half mad with joy. "I can love thee yet for a long time. My life is thine, and all that is of me comes from thee. A few drops of thy rich and noble blood, more precious and more potent than all the elixirs of the earth, have given me back life."

This scene haunted Daryl's memory, and inspired within him strange doubts in regards to Charlotte. Why had she been rejuvenated with his blood? Why?

Slumber that evening transported Daryl back to his home, where he awakened with the thoughts that all which had occurred was but a dream again. Upon awakening in his bedroom, he beheld the deacon, graver and more anxious than ever. He gazed attentively at Daryl, and sorrowfully exclaimed: "Not content with losing your soul, you now desire also to lose your body. Wretched young man, into how terrible a plight have you fallen!"

TALES MY GRANDMOTHER TOLD ME

The tone in which he uttered these words powerfully affected Daryl, but in spite of its vividness even that impression was soon dissipated, and a thousand other cares erased it from his mind. Anyway, he was only dreaming, because he was not back in his home, but right beside his dear Charlotte in bed. Yet, he spent the day reflecting on his dream, thinking that there was something sorely amiss.

That evening, while looking into a mirror, he saw Charlotte behind him in the act of emptying a powder into the cup of spiced wine which she had long been in the habit of preparing for him. She handed him the cup. He took it, feigned to carry it to his lips, and then placed it on the nearest article of furniture as though intending to finish it at his leisure. Taking advantage of a moment when the fair one's back was turned, he threw the contents into a nearby flower pot, after which he retired to his chamber and went to bed, fully resolved not to sleep, but to watch and discover what should come of all this mystery.

He did not have to wait long, Charlotte entered in her nightdress, and then having removed her apparel, crept into bed and lay down beside him. When she felt assured that he was asleep, she bared his arm, and drawing a gold pin from her hair, commenced to murmur in a low voice: "One drop, only one drop! One ruby drop at the end of my needle. Since thou lovest me yet, I must not die! Ah, poor love! His beautiful blood, so brightly purple, I must drink it. Sleep, my only treasure! Sleep, my god, my child! I will do thee no harm; I will only take of thy life what I must to keep my own from being forever extinguished. But that I love thee so much, I could well resolve to have other lovers whose veins I could drain; but since I have known thee all other men have become hateful to me. Ah, the beautiful arm! How round it is! How white it is! How shall I ever dare to prick this pretty blue vein?"

And while thus murmuring she wept, and Daryl felt her tears raining on his arm as she clasped it with her hands. At last she took the resolve, slightly punctured him with her pin, and commenced to suck up the blood which oozed from the place. Although she swallowed only a few drops, the fear of weakening him soon seized her, and she carefully tied a little band around his arm; afterward, lovingly rubbing the wound. Daryl could barely comprehend what he was enduring. Still, he could not cease to love Charlotte, and he realized he would gladly of his own accord have given her all the blood she required to sustain her factitious life as he had plenteous veins, which would not have been so easily exhausted; and he would not have thought of bargaining for his blood, drop by drop. He would much rather have opened the veins of his arms and lovingly said to her: "Drink dear, and may my love infiltrate itself throughout your body together with my blood!" Furthermore, he carefully never mentioned the narcotic drink she had prepared for him, or the incident with the pin, and they continued to live in the most perfect harmony.

J. WAYNE FRYE

TALES MY GRANDMOTHER TOLD ME

Yet his adherence to principles taught by the church commenced to torment him more than ever, and he was at a loss to imagine what new penance he could invent in order to mortify and subdue his adherence to church propaganda with which he had been indoctrinated all his life. He saw so much hypocrisy in the church, but he, himself, refused to have any part of it. In the effort to avoid falling under the influence of these wearisome hallucinations, he strove to prevent himself from being overcome by sleep. He held his eyelids open with his fingers, and stood for hours sternly leaning upright against the wall, fighting sleep with all his might; but the dust of drowsiness invariably gathered upon his eyes at last, and finding all resistance was useless, as he would have to let his arms fall in the extremity of despairing weariness, and the current of slumber would again bear him away to Charlotte's arms.

His torment grew with each day, as he began to question his sanity. He wondered whether his life with Charlotte was an illusion or not. It had to be a dream. Then, he would look at his arm and see little pin pricks in it, and he knew it was not a dream. Or, was he perhaps pricking his own arm?

Finally, finding himself back at home, he called upon the deacon to visit him, and it was then that he lay out in detail all that had been occurring. The deacon said, "Real or imagined, you are in the throes of Satan's design on your soul. There is but one way by which you can obtain relief from this continual torment, and though it is an extreme measure it must be made use of; violent diseases require violent remedies. I know where Charlotte is dead and buried. It is necessary that we shall disinter her remains, and that you shall behold in how pitiable a state the object of your love is. Then you will no longer be tempted to lose your soul for the sake of an unclean corpse devoured by worms and ready to crumble into dust. That will assuredly restore you to yourself."

He was tired of his double life of being a chaste minister one minute and then participating in debauchery the next. He felt on the edge of a precipice ready to tumble into Satan's grasp, Daryl at once consented, desiring to ascertain beyond a doubt whether he had been the victim of delusion or reality. So, with disinterment tools in hand, they were off to the cemetery where Charlotte had been buried long ago.

After having directed the rays of the lantern they carried upon the inscriptions of several tombs, they came upon a crypt with Charlotte's family name inscribed. The door to the crypt was squeakily pried open with a crowbar. They trod through the cobwebs and dust until coming upon a great slab, half concealed by huge weeds that had grown up through the concrete, whereupon they deciphered the opening lines of the epitaph: *Be leery any who would disturb this woman's resting place, for dire consequences will ensue.*

"She is here and you shall see that all is an illusion once and for all time," muttered the deacon, and placing his lantern on the ground, he forced the point of the lever they brought with them under the edge of the stone and commenced to raise it and then ease it over to the side in a catty-cornered fashion so as to be able to see the final resting place for Charlotte. He bent over the coffin and proceeded to pry the coffin lid slowly but assuredly open. Darker and more silent than the night itself, Daryl stood by mesmerized and watched him do it, while he, streamed with sweat, panted, as his hard-coming breath seemed to have the harsh tone of a death rattle. He felt sadness as he had never felt before. "How," he thought, as he looked down upon her sweetness, "could this person be evil?" She had never engaged in any livid debaucheries with him, unless two people in love sharing coupling intimacies are considered evil. No, she had simply loved him as no one else before ever had.

Daryl noticed that there was something extremely grim and fierce in the deacon's intense zeal which lent him the audacious air of a demon, and his great aquiline face, with all its abominably stern features, brought out in strong relief by the intensely flickering lantern-light, had something fearsome in it which enhanced the unpleasantness. This caused an icy sweat upon Daryl's forehead in huge beads, and his hair stood up with a hideous fear. Within the depths of his own heart, Daryl felt that the act of the austere deacon was an abominable sacrilege; and he wished for a triangle of fire to rise up from below to reduce the deacon to cinders.

He watched with pounding heart as the deacon wrenched apart the coffin lid, and Daryl beheld Charlotte, perfectly preserved in all her beauty, her hands joined with her white winding shroud making one fold from her head to her feet. And then he saw it. There was one crimson drop sparkling like a speck of dew at the corner of her colourless mouth. It was a remnant of Daryl's blood. He finally realized she was a vampire!

In shock, Daryl watched the perfectly preserved corpse open its eyes, as the deacon shouted, "You abomination in the eyes of the church," as he raised the wooden stake he had brought with him, ready to plunge it deep into her chest.

Charlotte replied, "The abomination is your hypocrisy. I have never killed anyone or pointed the finger of condemnation. I have only borrowed the blood of the living. You do not borrow; you steal by passing a collection plate where the poor place what little they have in hopes of a bountiful life in the hereafter, because they are denied it in the here and now by the church and the privileged class who steal from them with impunity." Then, as the deacon rammed the stake toward her heart, she reached up and grabbed his wrist, holding it only a few centimetres from her heart. Meanwhile, Daryl rushed toward him, shoving him away from the woman, away from the vampire he loved!

The deacon stumbled backwards, hit his head on a pillar and fell forward on the stake he brought to slay a vampire, but instead the stake killed a hypocrite. Daryl looked down at Charlotte who beckoned him. He crawled into the coffin; resting in the arms of his lover, as she reached up and closed the coffin lid on the two lovers who would rest in each others arms for eternity.

J. WAYNE FRYE

Chapter 5
On the Boat of Life

Being young is not the panacea some think,
Many are prisoners to the desire for youth,
which makes us miss the boat of life.

By the side of a great river, whose stream formed the boundary to two countries lived an old ferryman and his wife. All the day, while she minded the house, he sat by the ferry, waiting to carry travellers across; or, when no travellers came, and he had his boat free, he would cast drag-nets along the bed of the river for fish. Except for the food which he was able thus to procure at all times, he and his wife might well have starved, for travellers were generally few and very far between, and often they disgustingly grudged him the few dollars he asked for ferrying them; and now he had grown so old and feeble that when the river was in flood he could scarcely ferry the boat across, and continually he feared a younger and stronger man should come and take his place, and the bread from his mouth, for in the nation in which he lived, there was no concern for the aged, no attempt to make their declining years sanguine. Oh, how he longed for youth!

Like so many older people in this country where he lived, he had been conditioned to think God would always provide. The only trouble with that approach was that God had far too many people to look after, as the world then, as now, was run by the few at the expense of the many.

TALES MY GRANDMOTHER TOLD ME

One morning, it being the first day of the year, the ferryman going down to his boat, found that during the night it had been loosed from its moorings and taken across the river, where it now lay fastened to the further bank.

"Wife," said he "I can remember this same thing happening a year ago and every year before that. Who is this traveller who comes once a year, like a thief in the night, and crosses without asking me to ferry him over?

"Perhaps he just did not want to wake us and left a coin in the boat," his wife said.

"Never have before," he said as he picked up a paddle pole and boarded the small one man boat he kept by the water. He got to the other side quickly and looked down at the keel of the boat and saw the mark of a man's bare foot driven deep into the wood; but there was no coin or other trace to show who it might be.

Time went on; the old ferryman was all bowed down with age, and his body was racked with pain. So slow was he now in making the passage across the stream that all travellers who knew those parts took a road higher up the bank, where a stronger, younger ferryman had sat up shop.

Winter came. Hunger and want pressed hard at the old man's door. On the day before New Year's Eve, while he drew his net along the stream, he felt the shock of a great fish striking against the meshes down below, and presently, as the net came in, he saw a shape like living silver, leaping and darting to and fro to find some way of escape. Up to the bank he brought it, a great gasping fish.

J. WAYNE FRYE

When he was about to kill it, he saw, to his astonishment, tears running out of its eyes that gazed at him and seemed to reproach him for his cruelty. As he drew back, the fish said: "Why should you kill an old fish like me?"

The old man, altogether bewildered at hearing himself thus addressed by a fish, answered with surprise, "Since I and my wife are hungry, and God gave you to be eaten, I have good reason for killing you."

The fish replied, "I could give you something worth far more than a meal, if you would spare my life."

"My wife and I are old," said the ferryman, "and want only to end our days in peace. Today we are hungry, so what can be better for us than a meal which will give us strength for tomorrow, which is the New Year?"

The fish said, "Someone comes once a year and unfastens your boat, and ferries himself and another traveller over, and you know nothing of it until the morning, when you see the craft moored out yonder by the further bank. However, when you go back to your hut at night to sleep, I am here in the water, and I see what goes on."

"What goes on, then?" asked the old man, very curious to know who the strange traveller might be.

"Ah," said the fish, "if you could only catch him in your boat, he could give you something you might wish for! I tell you this. You and your wife keep watch in the boat all night, and when he comes, and he has ferried into mid-stream, where he cannot escape, then throw your net over him and hold him till he pays you for all the ferrying he stole."

"How shall he pay me, because he has been doing this for years without even one payment?

"Make him take you to the Land of Returning Time. There, at least, you can end your days in peace and in youthfulness."

"What is the Land of Retuning Time?" asked the old man.

"It is a land that will offer you happiness, giving you what you wish for – youth."

The old man said, "You have told me a strange thing, and since I mean to act on it I suppose I must let you go. If you have deceived me, trust that I shall see you may yet die a cruel death."

The fish answered, "Do as I tell you, and you shall die a happy man." And, saying this he slipped down into the water and disappeared.

The ferryman went back to his wife without sustenance, and said to her, "Wife, bring a net, and come down into the boat!" And he told her the story of the fish and how the fish apparently knew the yearly traveller who had not paid them for nigh on to fifty years.

They sat long together under the dark bank, looking out over the quiet and cold moonlit waters, until the midnight hour. The air was chilled, and to keep themselves warm they covered themselves over with the net and lay down in the bottom of the boat. It was the very hour when the old year dies and the New Year is born.

J. WAYNE FRYE

TALES MY GRANDMOTHER TOLD ME

Before they well knew that they had been asleep, they started to feel the rocking of the boat, and found themselves out upon the broad waters of the river. And there in the fore-part of the boat, clear and sparkling in the moonlight, stood a naked man of shining silver with a stoop shouldered old woman. He was bending upon the pole of the boat, and his long hair fell over it right down into the water. The old couple rose up quietly, and unwinding themselves from the net, threw it over the silver man, over his head, hands and feet, and dragged him down into the bottom of the boat along with the old lady.

The old man caught the ferry pole, and heaved the boat still into the middle of the stream. As he did so, a gentle shock came to his heart. Feebly it fluttered and sank low. "Oh, wife!" sighed the old man, and reached out his hand for hers as the silver man lay still in the folds of the net with the old woman by his side, and looked at them with a wise and quiet gaze. "What would you have of me?" he asked, with a far off and low voice.

They replied, "Take us into the Land of Returning Time."

The silver man said: "That is where I am taking this lady and have taken passengers for nigh on 50 years now. However, as I have told her, only once can you go there and once return."

They both answered, "We wish once to go there, and once return."

So he promised them that they should have the whole of their request, and they unloosed him and the old woman from the net, and landed altogether on the further bank of the river. Up a long hill they went, following the track of the silver man and old woman. Presently they reached its crest, and there before them lay all the howling winter.

The silver man turned his face and looked back, and his face became all young, ruddy and bright as did the old lady's face The ferryman and his wife gazed at them, both speechless at the wonderful change. He took their hands, making them turn the way by which they had come; below their feet was a black gulf, and beyond and away lay nothing but dark starless air.

"Now," said their guide, "you have but to step forward one step, and you shall be in the Land of Returning Time, along with me and my friend here whom I am also bringing to that land."

They loosed hold of his hands, clasped one another's hands and at one step upon what seemed a gulf beneath their feet, finding themselves in a green and flowery land. There were perfumed valleys and grassy hills, whose crops stretched down before the breeze; thick fleecy clouds crossed above their heads, and amid the blue air rang the shrill trilling of birds. Behind lay, fading mistily as a dream, the bare world they had left with the boat bouncing up and down tied up to the pier, and fast on his forward road, growing small to them from a distance, went the silver man and the old lady, a shining point on the horizon. He turned his head and shouted back, "I take her to another place in this land, but be warned, as if you want to return to your old life and old world, your ferry sails at dawn.

TALES MY GRANDMOTHER TOLD ME

The ferryman and his wife looked, and saw youth in each other's faces beginning to peep out through the furrows of age. The deep, dark lines began to melt away like ice-cream in the noonday sun. Each step they took made them grow younger and stronger as years fell from them like worn-out rags as they went down into the valley of the Land of Returning Time. How fast time returned. Each step made the change of a day, and every kilometre brought them five years back towards youth.

When they came down to the streams that ran in the bed of the valley, the ferryman and his wife felt their prime return to them. He saw the gold come back into her locks, and she the brown into his. Their lips became open to laughter and song. "Oh, how good," they cried, "to have lived all our lives poor to come at last to this!"

They drank water out of the streams, and tasted the fruit from the trees that grew over them; until presently, being tired from mere joy, they lay down in the grass to rest. They slept hand within hand and cheek against cheek, and, when they woke, found themselves quite young again, just at the age when they were first married in the years gone by. The ferryman started getting up and felt the desire of life strong in his blood. "Come!" he said to his wife, "or we shall become too young with lingering here. Now we have regained our youth, let us go back into the world once more!"

His wife hung upon his hand, "Are we not happy enough," she asked, "As it is? Why should we return?"

"But," he cried, "we shall grow too young; now we have youth and life at its best. Let us return! Time goes too fast with us. We are in danger of it carrying us away into childhood when we did not know each other."

She said nothing in return, but followed him towards the way by which they had entered, as he was desperately trying to make the boat before dawn came. And yet, in spite of her wish to remain, she went with him to the top of the hill, where they had parted ways with the silver man who had brought them so much happiness.

They suddenly looked at each and realized they had morphed into boy and girl again. "We have stayed here too long!" said the ferryman, and pressed on, hurriedly trying to make the boat that was moored below, his ferry boat that could take them back to where they had struggled but at least knew they would always have each other if not any riches.

"Oh, the birds," sighed she, "and the flowers, and the grassy hills to run on; we are leaving them behind!"

But the boy had the wish for a man's life, for their old life and urged her on. Still, with every rushed step they grew younger and younger. At length, now two young adults, they came to the border of that enchanted land, and saw beyond a world bleak and wintry, but they both knew that soon they would not be together, because they were going back, back, back in time until they would be but babes, and not be with one another. Only a further step was wanted to bring them face to face once more with the hard battle of life, but it was a step they wanted to take now, because they realized what had happened. They could find youth, but in finding it they could lose one another.

Tears rose the wife's eyes, as she said, "If we go, we can never return!"

"But," replied the ferryman, "if we stay, we will not be together. We did not meet until our teens. Can you not see what is happening?"

She then looked at him and said, "Yes, yes, we will lose each other, and that is a fate worse than growing old."

Now, with tears in his eyes, the old ferryman said, "I was tempted by that infernal fish that fooled me, and most of all by the silver man, who tempted both of us with the idea of youth. How foolish we were, because we stood to lose something more precious than youth. We could lose each other. I talked to you of being young. Don't you see what all that has meant? I am returning to being a little boy, and you are returning to being a little girl. How horrible it would be to return to being a boy and a girl without the life of a boy or a girl. Being young means bondage in so many ways. There is no agony of departure from this place. I want to return to our old home and old life and never look back with nostalgia for this place. I have now conquered the fear that possessed me. Not the fear of that hasty look round, the sudden plunge headlong and the giddy shock of hard, cold water, the river itself entering my lungs, rising in my throat, tossing me upon my back with my arms out-flung, as I hear the sob strangled in my chest and the blood leave me, but the real fear of the certain knowledge that there was a chance of losing you. If I have you, I have everything. With you I am the richest man in the world."

The two of them, holding hands, walked down to the boat and climbed aboard to return to their old life, a life that now was more precious and valued. On the shore was the silver man, waving at them and smiling, as they embraced and sailed home on the boat of life.

TALES MY GRANDMOTHER TOLD ME

CHAPTER 6
THE LEATHER STRAP OF HORROR

Until dawn from God knows where,
Beneath dark birds that filled the air,
Like one who did not hear or care,
Under a covering blood-red cloud,
A dark coach came pounding alone,
And drove through flesh and bone,
Carrying corpses as cold as stone.
Gallop dark coach into the black night,
As ghosts take deathly flight!

"The circumstances I relate to you my grandson," said my grandmother as she rocked in her chair, "have truth to recommend them. They happened. I know that for sure. Fifty years have gone by without me sharing this tale with anyone. During those years I have told the story to but one other person. I tell it now with a reluctance which I find it difficult to overcome. All I entreat, meanwhile, is that you will abstain from forcing your own conclusions. I want nothing explained away. I desire no arguments. My mind on this subject is quite made up, and, having the testimony of my own senses to rely upon, I prefer to abide by it. So, I tell you now of the phantom coach."

Perry Hunt had been hunting all day but bagged nothing. The wind was due east; the month, December; the place, a bleak wide moor in the far north of Carolina. And Perry had lost his way. It was not a pleasant place in which to lose one's way, with the first feathery flakes of a coming snowstorm just fluttering down. Perry stared anxiously into the gathering darkness, where the purple moorland melted into a range of low hills, some ten or twelve kilometres distant. Not the faintest smoke-wreath, not the tiniest cultivated patch, or fence or animal-track met his eyes in any direction. There was nothing to do but to walk on, and take his chance of finding what shelter he could, because he had walked far from where he had foolishly left his horse loosely tied to a tree when he went into the forest in search of game. He had returned and the horse had loosed itself and, no doubt, made its way to who knows where. So, he shouldered his rifle once again, and pushed wearily forward, for he had been on foot since an hour after daybreak, and had eaten nothing since breakfast.

Meanwhile, the snow began to come down with ominous steadiness and the wind picked up. After this, the cold became more intense, and the night came rapidly up. Perry felt great trepidation with the darkening sky, and his heart grew heavy as he thought how his young wife was already watching through the window of their little apartment above the inn in town, and thought of all the suffering in store for her throughout the weary night, because he had become lost. They had been married four months, and, having spent their autumn in the Piedmont area of North Carolina, were now lodging in a little village just outside of Asheboro, North Carolina. They were very much in love, and, of course, very happy. They were on an extended honeymoon, because Perry, a fairly successful writer, had been given a contract to write his fourth novel, and; thereby, combined a honeymoon with writing his next book. This morning, when they parted, she had implored him to return before dusk, and he had promised her that he would. What would he not have given to have kept his word?

As weary as he was, he felt that with a supper, an hour's rest, and a guide, he might still get back to her before midnight, if only guide and shelter could be found. And all this time the snow fell and the night thickened. He stopped and shouted every now and then, but his shouts seemed only to make the silence deeper. Then a vague sense of uneasiness came upon him, and he began to remember stories of travellers who had walked on and on in the falling snow until, wearied out, they were fain to lie down and sleep their lives away. Would it be possible, he thought, to keep on thus through all the long dark night? Would there not come a time when his limbs must fail and his resolution give way? How hard to die just now, when life lay all so bright before him. He shouted again, louder and longer, and then listened eagerly. Was his shout answered, or did he only fancy that he heard a far-off cry? He shouted again and again. Echoes followed. Then a wavering speck of light came suddenly out of the dark, shifting, disappearing and growing momentarily nearer and brighter. Running towards it at full speed, he found himself, to his great joy, face to face with an old man and a lantern.

"Thank God!" was the exclamation that burst involuntarily from his lips.

Blinking and frowning, the old man lifted his lantern and peered into Perry's face. "Thank God for what?"

"Well, for you," Perry replied. "I began to fear I should be lost in the snow."

"Eh, then, folks do get cast away hereabouts from time to time, but believe me, in this damnable place, no God can be found. This is a place where darkness rules both day and night?"

"What do you mean?" asked Perry.

"Never mind," he replied with some hesitation. "Just the ramblings of an old man. I hope you never find out what I mean. Come," he said as he turned and looked back over his shoulder, "follow me at your own peril."

Perplexed by what the old man had said; nonetheless, Perry ignored the comment and followed, asking "How far from here to Asheboro?"

A far piece, my friend," replied the old man as the two trudged onward. "In this weather and on foot, I'd say maybe you could make it by daybreak, but I wouldn't try it."

"Is there no other town nearby?"

"Franklinville is no more than thirty minutes by a buckboard with a swift horse pulling it, but, again, in this weather I wouldn't recommend it."

"Where do you live, then?"

"Out yonder," the old man said, with a vague jerk of the lantern.

"You're going home, I presume?" asked Perry.

"Maybe I am."

"Then I'm going with you."

The old man shook his head, and rubbed his nose reflectively. "It ain't no use. He won't let you in."

"We'll see about that," Perry replied, briskly. "Who is he?"

"The master."

"Who is the master?"

"Believe me, you don't want to know," was the unceremonious reply.

"Well, well; you lead the way, and I'll persuade the master to give me shelter and a bit of supper tonight."

"Eh, you can try him!" muttered the reluctant guide; and, still shaking his head, he hobbled, gnome-like, away through the falling snow. A large dark mass loomed up presently out of the darkness, and a huge dog rushed out, barking furiously.

"Is this the house?" Perry asked.

"Aye, it's the house." And he fumbled in his pocket for the key.

Perry drew up close behind him, prepared to lose no chance of entrance, and saw in the little circle of light shed by the lantern that the door was heavily studded with iron nails, like the door of a prison. In another minute he had turned the key and Perry had pushed past him into the house.

Once inside, Perry looked round with curiosity, and found himself in a great raftered hall, which served, apparently, a variety of uses. One end was piled to the roof with corn, like a barn. The other was stored with flour-sacks, many agricultural implements, casks, and all kinds of miscellaneous lumber; while from the beams overhead hung rows of hams and bunches of dried herbs for winter use. In the centre of the floor stood some huge object gauntly dressed in a dingy wrapping-cloth, and reaching half way to the rafters. Lifting a corner of this cloth, Perry saw, to his surprise, a telescope of very considerable size, mounted on a rude movable platform, with four small pin-like wheels. The tube was made of painted wood, bound round with bands of metal rudely fashioned. While Perry was examining the instrument, a bell rang sharply.

"That's for you," said the old man with a malicious grin. "Yonder's his room," he offered reluctantly as he pointed to a low black door at the opposite side of the hall. Perry crossed over, rapped somewhat loudly, and went in, without waiting for a formal invitation. A huge, white-haired old man rose slowly from a table covered with books and papers, and confronted him sternly. "Who are you?" he said. "How came you here? What do you want?"

"Perry Hunt, writer, and I came on foot across through the vast forest near here. I am weary from the walk and storm. Could I have a bit to eat and maybe a place to lie down until the storm subsides?"

He bent his bushy brows into a portentous frown. "Mine is not a house of entertainment," he said, haughtily. "Jacob, how dare you admit this stranger?"

"I didn't admit him," grumbled the old man. "He followed me over the way, and shouldered his way in before me. I'm no match for a man his size."

"And pray, sir, by what right have you forced an entrance into my house?"

"The same by which I should have clung to your boat, if I were drowning, the right of self-preservation."

"Self-preservation?" replied the disgusted man.

"There's almost half-a-foot of snow on the ground already, sir" Perry replied, "and it would be deep enough to cover my body before daybreak."

The man strode to the window, pulled aside a heavy black curtain, and looked out. "It is true," he said. "You can stay, if you choose, till morning. Jacob, serve him supper."

With this he waved Perry to a seat, resumed his own, and became at once absorbed in the studies from which he had been disturbed. He was a strange man indeed.

Perry placed his gun in a corner, drew a chair to the hearth, and examined the quarters at leisure. Smaller and less incongruous in its arrangements than the hall, this room contained, nevertheless, much to awaken curiosity. The floor was carpet-less. The whitewashed walls were in parts scrawled over with strange diagrams, and in others covered with shelves crowded with instruments, the uses of which were unknown to Perry. On one side of the fireplace stood a bookcase filled with dingy folios; on the other, a small pump organ, fantastically decorated with painted carvings of medieval saints and devils. Through the half-opened door of a cupboard at the further end of the room, Perry saw a long array of geological specimens, surgical preparations and jars filled with chemicals, while on the mantelshelf beside him, amid a number of small objects, stood a model of the solar system, a small battery and a microscope. Every chair had its burden. Every corner was heaped high with books. The very floor was littered over with maps, papers, tracings and lumber of all conceivable kinds.

Perry stared about with an amazement increased by every fresh object upon which his eyes chanced to rest. So strange a room he had never seen; yet seemed it stranger still, to find such a room in a lone farmhouse amid the wild and solitary place deep in the woods. Over and over again, he looked from his host to his surroundings and from his surroundings back to his host, asking himself who and what he could be? His head was singularly fine; but it was more the head of a poet than of a philosopher, broad in the temples, prominent over the eyes, and clothed with a rough profusion of perfectly coiffed white hair. There were deep lines about the mouth, and stern, very deep furrows in the thick brow. There was an intense concentration of expression.

As Perry was observing him, the door opened, and Jacob brought in the supper. His master then closed his book, rose, and with more courtesy of manner than he had yet shown, invited Perry to the table where there sat a dish of ham and eggs, a loaf of brown bread and a bottle of sherry.

TALES MY GRANDMOTHER TOLD ME

While Perry dined on a delightful meal, his host sat down to his own supper, which consisted, primitively, of a jug of milk and a bowel of soup. They ate in silence, and, when they were finished, Jacob removed the tray. Then Perry pushed his chair back to the fireside. His host, somewhat to his surprise, did the same, and turning abruptly towards him, said, "Sir, I have lived here in strict seclusion for many years. During that time, I have not seen any strange faces, and I have not read a single newspaper. You are the first stranger who has crossed my threshold for more than four years. Will you favour me with a few words of information respecting the outer world?

"I am heartily at your service," replied Perry.

Perry's host bent his head in acknowledgment; leaned forward, with his elbows resting on his knees and his chin supported in the palms of his hands; stared fixedly into the fire; and proceeded to question him with inquiries related chiefly to scientific matters, with the later progress of which, as applied to the practical purposes of life, he was almost wholly unacquainted. No student of science himself, Perry replied as well as his dearth of information permitted; but the task was far from easy, and he was much relieved when, passing from interrogation to discussion, he began pouring forth his own conclusions upon the facts which he had been attempting to place before him. He talked, and Perry listened spellbound. He had never heard anything like it. Familiar with all systems of all philosophies, subtle in analysis, bold in generalisation, he poured forth his thoughts in an uninterrupted stream, and, still leaning forward in the same moody attitude with his eyes fixed upon the fire, wandered from topic to topic, from speculation to speculation, like an inspired dreamer. From practical science to mental philosophy were transitions which, however bewildering in their variety and scope, seemed easy and harmonious upon his lips as sequences in music. By-and-by, he passed on to that field which lies beyond the boundary line of even conjectural philosophy, as he spoke of the soul and its aspirations; of the spirit and its powers; of second sight; of prophecy; of those phenomena which, under the names of ghosts, spectres and supernatural appearances, have been denied by the sceptics and attested by the credulous, of all ages.

"The world," he said, "grows hourly more and more sceptical of all that lies beyond its own narrow radius; and our men of science foster the fatal tendency. They condemn as fable all that resists experiment. They reject as false all that cannot be brought to the test of the laboratory or the dissecting-room. Against what superstition have they waged so long and obstinate a war, as against the belief in apparitions? And yet what superstition has maintained its hold upon the minds of men so long and so firmly? Show me any fact in physics, in history, in archaeology, which is supported by testimony so wide and so various. Attested by all races of men, in all ages, and in all climates, by the soberest sages of antiquity, by the Christian, the Pagan, this phenomenon is treated as a nursery tale by the philosophers of our century. Circumstantial evidence weighs heavily with them as a feather in the balance. The comparison of causes with effects, however valuable in physical science, is put aside as worthless and unreliable. The evidence of competent witnesses, however conclusive in a court of justice, counts for nothing as he who believes in fanciful tales is a dreamer or a fool."

He spoke with bitterness, and, having said thus, relapsed for some minutes into silence. Presently he raised his head from his hands, and added, with an altered voice and manner, "I, sir, paused, investigated, believed, and was not ashamed to state my convictions to the world. I, too, was branded as a fool, held up to ridicule by my contemporaries, and hooted from that field of science in which I had laboured with honour during all the best years of my life. These things happened many years ago. Since then, I have lived as you see me living now, and the world has forgotten me, as I have forgotten the world. You have my history."

"It is a very sad one," Perry murmured, scarcely knowing what to answer.

"It is a very common one," he replied. "I have only suffered for the truth, as many a better and wiser man has suffered before me. The truth is a rare commodity in the world. People are easily fooled and only hear what they want to hear, only hear that which substantiates their beliefs, and their beliefs are manipulated by charlatans." He then slowly rose, as if desirous of ending the conversation and went over to the window.

TALES MY GRANDMOTHER TOLD ME

"It has ceased snowing," he observed, as he dropped the curtain, and came back to the fireside.

"Ceased!" Perry exclaimed, starting eagerly to his feet. "Oh, if it were only possible, but no! It is hopeless. Even if I could find my way, I could not walk far on the ground laden with snow in the darkness."

"Walk tonight!" repeated the host. "What are you thinking of?"

"Of my wife," Perry replied, impatiently. "Of my young wife, who does not know that I have lost my way, and who is at this moment breaking her heart with suspense and terror."

"Where is she?"

"Near Asheboro."

"Asheboro," he echoed stoically. "Not a problem really, as the night mail from the north, which changes horses at a nearby stable, passes within five kilometres of this spot, and will be due at a certain crossroad in about an hour and a quarter. If Jacob were to go with you across the forest, and put you into the old coach road, you could find your way, I suppose, to where it joins the new one? The coach slows to get over the pass and you could flag it down."

"That would be great!" offered Perry.

"I am off to bed, now," said the host abruptly as he summoned Jacob and explained what must be done.

Perry would have thanked him for his hospitality, and would have shaken hands, but he had turned away before he could finish a sentence. In another minute, Perry had traversed the hall,

Jacob had locked the outer door behind him and they were out in a sea of white powder.

Although the wind had fallen, it was still bitterly cold. Not a star glimmered in the black vault-like sky overhead. Not a sound, save the rapid crunching of the snow beneath their feet, disturbed the heavy stillness of the night. Jacob, not too well pleased with his mission, shambled on before Perry in sullen silence, his lantern in his hand and his shadow at his feet. Perry followed, with his gun over his shoulder while he was in deep thought about his most unusual host. His eloquent voice yet rang in his ears while still holding his ears in imaginative captivation. His still excited brain retained whole sentences and parts of sentences, troops of brilliant images, and fragments of splendid reasoning in the very words in which his host had uttered them. Musing thus over what he had heard, and striving to recall a lost link here and there, he strode on at the heels of his guide, absorbed and unobservant. Presently, at the end of only a few minutes, Jacob came to a sudden halt, and said as he pointed with somewhat of a smirk on his face into the distance, "Yon's your road. Keep the stone fence to your right hand, and you can't fail of the way."

"This, then, is the old coach-road?"

"Ay, 'tis the old coach-road."

"And how far do I go, before I reach the cross-roads?"

"Nigh upon three kilometres."

Perry pulled out his purse, and suddenly Jacob became more communicative. "The road's a fair road enough," said he, "for foot passengers. You'll mind where the wall by the curve is broken away. It's never been mended since the accident."

"What accident?"

"Eh, the night mail coach pitched right over into the valley at least 2000 feet below."

"Horrible! Were many lives lost?"

"All. Four were found dead, and t'other two died next morning."

"How long is it since this happened?"

"Many, many a year ago, a long, long time."

"I'll be careful then. Good night."

"Good night, sir, and thanks," he said as he pocketed the money handed him by Perry, turned and walked away.

Perry watched the light of his lantern until it disappeared, and then turned to pursue his way alone. There was no longer the slightest difficulty, for, despite the dead darkness overhead, the line of stone fence showed distinctly enough against the pale gleam of the snow. How silent it seemed now, with only his footsteps to listen to; how silent and how solitary. An incredibly strange disagreeable sense of loneliness stole over Perry, making him walk faster. Meanwhile, the night air seemed to become colder and colder, and though he walked fast he found it impossible to keep himself warm. His feet were like ice. He lost sensation in his hands and breathed with difficulty, as though, instead of traversing a quiet north country highway, he was actually scaling the uppermost heights of some gigantic mountain. This last symptom became presently so very distressing that he was forced to stop for a few minutes, and lean against the stone fence. As he did so, he chanced to look back up the road, and there, to his infinite relief, he saw a distant point of light, like the gleam of an approaching lantern. At first he concluded that Jacob had retraced his steps and followed him, but even as the conjecture presented itself, a second light flashed into sight, a light evidently parallel with the first, and approaching at the same rate of motion. It needed no second thought to show Perry that these must be the carriage-lamps of some solitary vehicle, though it seemed strange that any such vehicle should take a road professedly disused and dangerous. There could be no doubt, however, of the fact, for the lamps grew larger and brighter every moment, and he even fancied he could already see the dark outline of the carriage between them. It was coming up very fast, and quite noiselessly, the snow being nearly a foot deep under the wheels.

Then the body of the vehicle became distinctly visible behind the lamps. It looked strangely lofty. A sudden suspicion flashed upon him. Was it possible that he had passed the spot where he was told to wait for the coach, and could this be the very coach which he had come to meet but somehow missed it? There was no need to ask himself that question a second time, for here it came round the bend of the road, guard and driver, one outside passenger, and four steaming horses, all wrapped in a soft haze of light, through which the lamps blazed out, like a pair of fiery meteors.

He jumped forward, waved his hat, and shouted. The mail coach came down at full speed and passed him. For a moment he feared that he had not been seen or heard, but it was only for a moment. The coachman pulled up; the guard, muffled to the eyes in capes and comforters, and apparently sound asleep in the rumble, neither answered his hail nor made the slightest effort to dismount; the outside passenger did not even turn his head. So, without words, Perry reached over and opened the door for himself, and looked in. There were but three travellers inside, so he stepped in, shut the door, slipped into the vacant corner, and congratulated himself on his good fortune.

The atmosphere of the coach seemed, if possible, colder than that of the outer air, and was pervaded by a singularly damp and disagreeable smell. He looked around at his fellow-passengers. They were all three men and all completely silent. They did not seem to be asleep, but each leaned back in his corner of the vehicle, as if absorbed in his own reflections. Perry attempted to open a conversation with the man right across from him. "How intensely cold it is tonight," he said.

The passenger lifted his head, looked at Perry, but made no reply, so Perry continued, "The winter seems to have begun in earnest."

Although the corner in which the man sat was so dim that Perry could distinguish none of his features very clearly, he saw that his piercing eyes were sternly focused on him. Still, the man was silent. It was obvious the man was not going to converse with him. Perry shivered from head to foot, and, turning to his left-hand neighbour, asked if he had any objection to an open window due to the foul smell in the coach? He neither spoke nor stirred.

Perry repeated the question somewhat louder, but with the same result. Then he lost patience, and let the sash up slightly without permission. As he did so, the leather strap broke in his hand, and he observed that the sash was covered with a thick coat of intense mildew, the accumulation, apparently, of many years. His attention being thus drawn to the condition of the coach, he examined it more narrowly, and saw by the uncertain light of the outer lamps that it was in the last stage of dilapidation. Every part of it was not only out of repair, but in a condition of decay. The sashes splintered at a touch. The leather fittings were crusted over with mould, and the woodwork was rotting. The floor was almost breaking away beneath his feet. The whole machine, in short, was foul with dampness and outright decay.

He turned to the third passenger, whom he had not yet addressed, and hazarded one more remark. "This coach," he said, "is in a deplorable condition. The regular mail coach, I suppose, is under repair?"

The passenger moved his head slowly, and looked Perry in the face, without speaking a word. Perry turned ice cold from the gaze. The man's eyes glowed with a fiery unnatural lustre. His face was livid as the face of a corpse. His bloodless lips were drawn back as if in the agony of death.

Perry's sight had by this time become used to the gloom of the coach, and he could see with tolerable distinctness. He turned to his opposite passenger. He, too, was staring intently at Perry, with the same startling pallor on his face, and the same stony glitter in his eyes. Perry passed his hand across his brow. He turned to the passenger on the seat beside his own, and what he saw for the first time was that he was no living man—that none of them were living men, like himself. A pale phosphorescent light, the dull light of putrefaction, played upon their awful faces; upon their hair, dank with the dews of the grave; upon their clothes, earth-stained and dropping to pieces; upon their hands, which were the decaying hands of corpses long buried. Only their eyes seemed alive, alive with the coldness of the grave.

A shriek of terror, a wild unintelligible cry for help and mercy burst from Perry's lips as he flung himself against the door and strove in vain to open it. He could not!

In that single instant, brief and vivid as a landscape beheld in the flash of summer lightning, Perry saw the moon shining down through a rift of stormy cloud, and all the passengers were staring at him and smiling. He screamed with terror, as he tried opening the door, so that he might leap from the coach. Oh, but he could not, because he was locked inside a coach of horror, a coach that was destined to take the same route again and again and relive that horrible accident. As they tumbled over the side, Perry's screams reverberated through the dark night.

J. WAYNE FRYE

TALES MY GRANDMOTHER TOLD ME

It seemed as if years had gone by when Perry awoke one morning from a deep sleep, and found his wife watching by his bedside. She related to him how he had fallen over a precipice, close against the junction of the old coach-road and the new Spiro Road to Asheboro, and had only been saved from certain death by lighting upon a deep snowdrift that had accumulated at the ledge of the cliff. He must have somehow lost his way on the road, and become so disoriented that he simply walked over the cliff by mistake, but fortunately landed on a ledge maybe fifty feet below. In this snowdrift on the ledge, two men riding horses to town had heard sobbing below and found his nearly lifeless body. They carried him across their horses to town and brought a doctor to his aid. The doctor found him in a state of raving delirium, with a broken arm and a compound fracture of the skull. The letters in his pocket showed his name and address. Thus, he was brought home, where he came out of danger at last. The place of his fall was precisely that at which several frightful accidents had occurred, with people being found at the bottom of the cliff over a period of many years, and it seemed that Perry was the second person to survive, and the other survivor had wound up in an asylum, as he insisted he had been to a cabin in the woods where an old white haired man and his servant had hosted him and then sent him on his way to face a horrible destiny apparently. He said he had been riding in a coach with dead men. However, no cabin or old man was ever found in any investigations of the accidents on that old road. Oh, and there were never any wagon wheel marks in the snow.

Taking a deep breath, Perry decided it would be best not to tell her what he had experienced. After all, it must have all been just an illusion. There was no old white haired man, no servant named Jacob, and no ghostly coach on the road. He smiled at his beloved wife and said, "All is O.K. now. I am with you and safe."

She got up, walked to the dresser, picked up something and walked back. She looked lovingly down at him and said, "Oh, here is something you were clinging to, something that no one could pry from your hand until you got back here and were put to bed. Nobody knows what it is." She extended her hand with the item, and placed it in his hand, as she asked, "What is it?"

With a look of horror, he said, as he fondled it, "This is a strap from a stage coach leather window."

TALES MY GRANDMOTHER TOLD ME

Chapter 7
To Live They Must Feed on the Living

Come to me in the night,
For I am a nocturnal creature.
Wake me with sweet kisses
And my sharp teeth will pierce
Your hollowed and willing throat,
And we shall love, and love,
Like the moon was our sun.

Again, grandmother rocked, as she said, "Love comes along at times when we least expect it, and often with people who can doom us, or doom our memories to carry that love and the things we did for it with us unto eternity. Such is the story Lon Hopkins, my dear old cousin. You must never reveal to him that I have shared this story with you, because people might think he should be in a mental intuition; or if not there, they might believe he should have long ago been hanged for murder."

Now that the incident is all over, it seems like a bad dream to him. But I have seen him look at Maria's picture for many years now, and I realize it couldn't have been a dream. Actually, it was only a few months ago that I sat in his den and glanced over at his desk, as he was looking at her picture, still lamenting the fact that his only real love had been gone nigh on to 50 years. You see, though only a girl of twelve, when the tragedy occurred, I had sat there all those years ago with him looking at the picture, wondering what could have happened to her. It was so long ago I may get the details a bit mixed up, but you see it had been six weeks since there had been any word from her, and she had promised to write as soon as she arrived in Europe. Considering that his future rested in her small hands, he had every right to be apprehensive, and although I was only twelve, I understood love, and felt so sorry for him. You see, they had grown up together, had lost their folks within a few years of each other and had been fond of each other the way kids are apt to be. Then the change came. It seemed he loved her, and she was still just fond of him. During their early college days at the University of North Carolina he sort of let things ride, but once they went on to graduate school at Duke University, he began to become pushy, to actually make a nuisance of himself professing his love for her. The next thing he knew, she had signed up with a student tour destined for Europe, and told him she would give him her answer in regards to his request to marry her when she returned. He had to be content with that, but couldn't help worrying. Maria was a strange girl who was withdrawn, dreamy and soft-hearted. Knowing that she was going to Transylvania, he was inclined to be uneasy, since it is the realm of gypsies, fortune tellers and the like. It is also the birthplace of many strange legends, and Maria claimed to be strongly psychic. As a matter of fact, she had foretold one or two things which were probably coincidental, like the death of her own parents, and then the death of Lon's parents in a horrible accident. She had dreamed these things.

TALES MY GRANDMOTHER TOLD ME

This seemingly psychic talent of hers led her into trouble on more than one occasion. I remember in her senior year at college she fell under the spell of a short, fat, greasy spook-reader with a strictly phony accent and all but gave her eye teeth away, until Lon realized something was amiss, got to the bottom of it, and dispatched the charlatan in rather unceremonious fashion. For that reason, he feared she might meet some unsavoury, unscrupulous person on her trip, and would have no one around to get her out of the scrape. When she didn't write at first, he let it go that she was busy. Finally, six weeks' silent treatment aroused his curiosity. It also aroused his nasty temper, and the next thing I knew he was on a plane bound for Romania. Within four hours after landing, he found her at a little inn in Transylvania, a quaint little place that looked as if it were made of gingerbread, and was surrounded by the huge, craggy Transylvania Mountain range.

His temper got the best of him when he saw her sitting in the pub with another student who had gone on the trip, Todd Hunter. Lon nearly shouted at her, "What's wrong, Maria? Why didn't you write?"

Her usually gay, shining brown eyes flashed angrily. "Why couldn't you leave me alone? I told you not to come after me. I came here so I could think this out. For God's sake, Lon, can't you see I wanted to think and be by myself?"

"But you promised to write," Lon persisted, wondering at the change in her, the impatience, and the extreme weight loss that was apparent.

"Maria has been studying much too diligently," Todd said slowly. "She's always tired lately. She hasn't been too well, either. Her throat bothers her."

Lon wanted to punch him as he looked at Maria and said, "So, you wanted to be alone. Then why are you with this jerk." Maria gave Lon a stern look, as he continued, "This guy's no good for you. Can't you see that? What do you know about him?"

She looked at Lon with an even sterner look, her eyes surprised and a little hurt. "All I have to know," she almost whispered. "I love him." She then looked out the window at the mountain in the distance, as she continued "I am going up Mount Călimanului tomorrow. There, right next to Bran Castle, is a small sanatorium. The doctor told me I must go away, and Todd has suggested this place. There Todd and I shall be married."

Lon was determined she was not going to marry someone about whom she knew absolutely nothing. She was much more ill than she knew he determined. He immediately assumed that Todd was undoubtedly after her money, as she was considerably well-off. Obviously she was once more being unduly influenced.

"I won't let you!" Lon warned. "Give it some more time. You needed time to consider my proposal and now after a measly six weeks travelling with this miscreant you are ready for marriage."

"How about me, Lon?" Todd interrupted. "You haven't asked me my feelings on the subject. I happen to love Maria dearly. Have I no say just because you're a childhood friend of hers?"

"Childhood friend! I was her whole family for years before she ever heard of you! I'll see you in hell before I let her marry you!" Lon shouted.

A perturbed Maria said, "That's enough, Lon! I've heard all I want to from you. I'm twenty-three, and if I choose to marry Todd, I'll do so and there's nothing you can do about it. Now, please go."

"O.K., Maria," said Lon, "if that's the way you want it. But I'm not through. If you won't protect yourself, I'll do it for you. I'd like to know more about the mysterious Todd, and I do wish, for your own sake, you'd do the same. I wouldn't care who you married, so long as you knew all about him. People just don't marry strangers; not if they're smart. You are not being smart. Ask about him. I dare you. Just do me one favour, don't marry him until I get back. Only a little while; give me a week. Just wait a little longer."

As Lon turned and left, while walking to the door he could feel Todd's smirk. He knew Maria would not wait.

Lon was gone back to the USA for a week. He had walked his legs off trying to track down information on the elusive Todd Hunter and discovered exactly nothing. All Todd's landlady could tell him was that he was unfriendly, terribly strange acting with an evil glare that made her feel incredibly uncomfortable every time she was around him, and that he slept all day and went out only at night.

He went directly, upon returning to Bran, Romania to Maria's apartment, and entered without knocking. They were waiting for him, her and Todd. When he saw her, he was shocked. She lay in Todd's arms, her body almost a skeleton. White and cold she was, like frozen milk just removed from a freezer. They were both dead.

How often thought Lon that he had been to a woman's funeral and looked at the corpse which had been all made up and said, "She's beautiful," but Maria was not beautiful at all. She was just a lifeless handful of decaying flesh hanging precariously on a skeleton. Their fair skins were faintly pink-tinted and their hair dishevelled. They sat so close on the sofa before the fire, his head resting in the hollow of her throat. They looked emaciated but peaceful and no lines marred their faces. Lon almost fancied he saw them breathing. And on Maria's third finger, left hand, was the ring, a thin, platinum band. He had won, and in winning somehow he had lost. How they had died and why they found each other and death at the same time, he assumed he would probably never know. He only knew one thing. He had to get away from there, quickly. He almost ran the distance to his hotel. He felt saltiness in his throat and realized that he had swallowed some tears that were running uncontrollably down both his cheeks into his partially opened mouth. Suddenly, he was sobbing like a baby.

He did not call the police. That would mean he would have to go back and watch them cover that emaciated body of the woman he loved, carry it away and submit it to untold indignities in order to ascertain the cause of death. The cleaning girl would find them in the morning and would notify the police.

However, it was not as simple as that. In the morning he found he couldn't shake off the guilt which possessed him. He phoned the building landlord where Maria was staying and told him he had failed to reach the two by phone, and that he was sure something was amiss. Would he please go to their flat and see if anything was wrong. He was amused. "Really, Mr. Hopkins, you must be mistaken. Miss Maria went out just an hour ago with her new husband. Surely you are jesting. Why she has never looked better. So happy. They have left for Bran Castle. They have also left you a note.

He told him he would be right over, and immediately went out and hailed a cabbie. He began to think he was losing his mind. He had seen them both dead. The landlord had seen them that morning, alive.

When he arrived, the landlord looked at him for a long moment, taking in his rough, dark-blue complexion, un-pressed clothes, red-rimmed eyes, then wagged a finger playfully, as she assumed he had a night of revelry and said, "Here is your letter."

He went where he would be undisturbed, to the reading room of the library on the same street as his flat. To the musty, oblong, dimly lit room whose threshold, sunshine and fresh air dared not cross. Without the saving warmth of sunlight or the fresh, clean relief of sweet-smelling air, he read. Read, inhaling the pungent, sour smell of the many old books that were all about. Read, and then doubted that he had read at all, but the blue ink on the white paper forced him to acknowledge its actuality. It had been written by Todd in a neat, scholar's script.

Dear Lon:

With Maria I have known the happiest days of my life. I want no more than that. I have no right to ask for more. Have we, any of us, a right to endless bliss on this earth? Hardly.

You thought of her welfare above all; for that I owe you some explanation. You must be patient, you must believe, and in the end, you must do as I ask. You must.

You wanted to know about me, of my life before Maria. It seems strange to think about it. There is no life without Maria. Still, there was a time when, for me, she didn't exist. I have been constantly going forward to the day when I would meet her, yet there was a time when I didn't know where I would find her, or even what her name would be! It was chance that brought us together. For me, good chance; for you, possibly ill chance; for Maria? Only she can say. A few years ago I was studying and the future held great things for me. Studying intensified for me. The folklore of Transylvania intrigued me. I delved into the Black Welsh tales, the mischievous fancies of the Irish, the English legends of the prowling werewolf. For me it was a relief from political science, which suddenly palled and which smacked of treason in the light of current events. My extracurricular research consumed the better part of my evenings. My books were and always have been a part of me, and as was to be expected, I overdid it. I studied too hard with too little let-up. Sometimes it seemed to me there was more truth to what I read than myth. It became somewhat of an obsession. Suddenly, one night, everything blacked out.

I came to in a sanatorium. I didn't know how I got there, but when they explained it to me, I laughed. I thought they were joking. When I tried to get up, to walk, I collapsed. Then I knew how bad it had been. I knew, too, I would have to go slowly.

It was there I met Eve. She was beautiful. Not like Maria, who is like a fragile, fair, spun-sugar angel. Eve was more earthy, with skin like ivory, creamy and rich and pale. Her coal-black hair she wore long and gathered in the back. She looked about twenty-five, but a streak of pure white ran back from each of her temples. She was the most striking woman I have ever met. I had never known anyone like her, nor have I since I saw her last.

You know how it is: the air of mystery about a woman makes a man like a kid again. She reminded me of a sleek, black cat, with her large, hazel eyes. I bumped into her one day on the veranda, and spent every day with her after that.

The doctors wanted me to take exercise, short walks and the like, and Eve went with me, but only at night. She struggled to keep up with me. The slightest effort tired her. She suffered from a rather nasty case of anaemia. She seldom smiled; the effort was probably too much for her. I saw her really smile only once.

We had been on one of our short nighttime hikes about the moonlit grounds, when she stumbled over a twig or a branch, I'm not sure which. Suddenly she was in my arms. Have you ever held a cloud in your arms? So light she was, it as like holding a feather. Oh, how cold she was. Her eyes held mine; it was almost uncanny. I have never been affected like that by a woman. Then I was kissing her; then a sharp sting, and I winced. There was the warm, salt taste of blood on my lips. I never knew how it happened. But she was smiling, her full mouth parted in the strangest smile I have ever seen. And those small white teeth gleamed; and in her eyes, which were all black pupils now, with the iris quite hidden, was desire, or something beyond desire. I couldn't define it then; now, I think I can. Her small, pink tongue darted over her lips, tasting, seeming to savour my blood that she had extracted.

I was frightened, for some indefinable reason. I wanted to get away from her, back inside the sanatorium. I grasped her arm roughly and we started back. We never mentioned the episode again, but neither of us ever forgot it. She intrigued me now, more than ever. The doctors were able to satisfy my curiosity somewhat. They told me she had been a patient for some four years. Some days she was better, some days worse. She needed rest, much rest. She slept all day every day, only awakening at night.

TALES MY GRANDMOTHER TOLD ME

Just when we became lovers, I scarcely remember. Things were happening so fast I could barely keep pace with them. There was magnetism about Eve which was compelling. I couldn't have resisted if I had wanted to, but anyway, I didn't want to resist.

I began to have long periods of lassitude, times when I would black out and remember nothing afterwards. And the dreams began. I would dream I was stroking a large, velvety-black cat, a cat with shining yellow eyes that looked at me as if they knew my every thought. I would stroke it continuously and it would nip me playfully. Then, one night the dream intensified. I was playing with the creature, caressing it gently, when all of a sudden its lips drew back in a snarl, and without warning it sprang at my throat and buried its fangs deep! I thought I could feel life being drawn from me; I screamed. The doctors told me afterwards that I was semi-conscious for days; that I had to be restrained. When I was well again, Eve came to see me. She was gentle and soothing. She held me close to her, and it was good to be alive and to belong to someone. I remember to this day what she wore. Black velvet lounging slacks, a low-necked amber satin blouse, caught at the "V" by a curiously wrought antique silver pin. It was round, small in diameter. In its centre was the carved figure of a serpent coiled to strike. Its eyes were deep amber topazes and its darting tongue was raised and set with a blood-red ruby. "What an unusual pin, Eve," I continued, "I've never seen you wear it before."

"No," she replied. "You see, my great-great grandmother was quite a wicked lady, to hear tell. She went in for witches' masses and the like. They say she poisoned her husband, a rather elderly and very childish man, for her lover, whom she subsequently married. Together they did away with relatives who stood in the way of their accumulating more money. This pin was the instrument of death."

Her slim fingers pressed the ruby tongue and the pin opened, revealing a space large enough to secrete powder. "Perhaps it was fate then that her devoted new husband tired of her once her fortune was assured him, took a young mistress for himself, and disposed of the unfortunate wife, using her own pin to perpetrate her murder with a deadly poison. But let's not discuss such unpleasant things, my dear. The important thing now is for you to get well quickly. I've missed you terribly, you know."

It was then I asked her to marry me. I knew I didn't really love her, but there seemed nothing to prevent our marriage. And she had gotten under my skin. She said she thought we should wait until I fully recovered.

She bent over me solicitously and I reached up to stroke that smooth black hair. It had a familiar feel to it that I couldn't quite place. Of course I had stroked it hundreds of times before, but it wasn't that. Then she looked straight at me, those large, glowing dark eyes boring into mine, and I knew. Knew and disbelieved at the same time. I froze where I lay, paralyzed by my fear; unable to make a sound. *"So you know,"* she whispered. *"It is well. I have marked you for my own these many months. Now that you know, you will not fight. You know what I am, or at least you can guess. This pin you admired so; it was mine three hundred years ago and it will always be mine!"*

Her lips were on mine. She had never kissed me like this. It was like the touch of hot ice, freezing, then searing, unendurable. I lay inert; I couldn't have moved if I wanted to. I could scarcely breathe. Then I felt the blood within me pounding, pulsing, beginning to answer in spite of myself. I tasted once more the warm, salty fluid on my lips. Eve's body was liquid in my arms; warm, heady, narcotizing. I felt the agonizing, dagger sharp pain in my throat and then darkness descended completely over me.

Have you ever wakened to a bright, sunny afternoon and heard yourself pronounced dead? They spoke in low, hushed tones. How unfortunate. Young fellow only thirty, dying so far away from his homeland. No family. Good thing he was well-set in life. This sudden anaemia was most extraordinary; fellow showed no signs of it previously. All he had really needed was rest. If he had recovered, that lovely Eve might have made both their lives happier, richer. Good of her to claim the body. She said she was going to inter it in the family vault up on Bran Mountain in Transylvania.

I heard them distinctly. I wanted to shout that I wasn't dead. I wanted to wake up from this horrible nightmare. I was alive. I knew I had to get out of there, some way; to get away from Eve, whom I now feared. They left to make arrangements.

The lassitude crept through me without warning; I dozed in spite of myself and then I heard Eve. "Todd," she said, "Get up, my dear."

There was a white mist before my eyes. I reached up to brush it away. It was not a mist; it was a cloth. I shivered. There was a creaking sound and then faint light. I saw where I was. I covered my face with my hands and sobbed. I tried to pray, but the words froze on my lips. I was in a coffin in a mausoleum! I had been buried alive!

"What am I?" I shrieked. "Where am I and what have you done?"

Standing over me was Eve. Her lips parted, showing the even white teeth, especially those slightly pointed incisors.

"Welcome, my dear," she said calmly. "You are now one of us; a revenant, even as I am, and to live you must feed on the living."

"It's not true!" I shouted. "This is all a crazy nightmare, part of my illness! You're not real! Nothing is real!"

"I'm quite real, Todd. To be trite, I am what I am, and have accepted it calmly, as you shall in time."

"No!" I cried.

She chuckled drily. "I'm afraid these things do happen. Make the best of it."

But I wouldn't; I refused to for a while. I would not feast on the blood of the living. Something within me fought, for a time.

Then, the awful hunger began. The tearing pangs of hunger that ordinary food wouldn't arrest. I fought it as long as I could. I lost. First it was small animals; animals that I loved. It was my life or theirs. Then there was a little girl; a dear little creature who might have been my child under different circumstances.

After the episode of the little girl, Eve left me. She had no further use for me, because she had wanted the child, too, and I had got it. I was now competition to be shunned. I was alone once again, alone and thoroughly miserable. I couldn't understand myself, my motives, so how could I expect someone else to understand?

I only knew what I was; nor could I rationalize on why I had become this way. I could only presume it had happened to others equally as innocent as myself of wrong-doing. In the daytime, I avoided the sunlight, and realized I was a creature of the night, because that was when I sought the blood of the living. I reproached myself; goodness knows I loathed myself and what I had to do in order to live. I wished I might really die, for I was tired, so frightfully tired and sick of it all. But I knew of no way to accomplish this, so I had to bear it all, fasting until my voracious, disgusting appetites got the better of me.

I decided to go to graduate school at Duke and there find information on my kind. It was there I met Maria. She told me, after we knew each other better, that she was doing her thesis on regional superstitions with emphasis on the history of vampirism. She found it terribly amusing, but at the same time frightening: Didn't I? I fear I saw nothing laughable about it, but I held my peace. Why I could have done a thesis for her that would have driven some mild-mannered professor completely out of his mind! I kept my knowledge to myself, though, but in the process of accumulating knowledge I discovered the one way vampires can be destroyed. I had seen it time and again in movies, but the truth was there in those musky old books. A vampire could be destroyed with a stake through its heart. Of course, the one thing left out in the movies was that the stake was only to render the vampire powerless to resist the final act that would kill the abdominal blood sucking creatures, decapitation and the burning of the head.

I do not know how it happened, but like a flash of sunshine in a darkened room I was in love with her. She made each day worth living. For the first time the hunger pangs ceased and I was certain I was cured. Perhaps, I thought, the whole thing was just a dream, and I was finally awake.

I felt then I had the right to tell her of my love, which I did when we took the trip to study in Romania. She looked infinitely sad. She wasn't certain, she said. She knew she was awfully fond of me, but she was confused. She had feelings for you, and was trying to make up her mind about you, whom she didn't want to hurt. I said I would wait up to and through eternity, if she wished.

Things went along peacefully then as I waited. We would walk for hours together, walk in complete silence and understanding. My strength seemed to be returning more day by day. We went far afield in search of material for her thesis. She would track down the minutest speck of hearsay, to get authenticity. One day, in our wanderings, I thoughtlessly let myself be led too near my resting place at Bran Castle. One of the locals mentioned a "place of horror" nearby and Maria wanted to investigate. I had no choice. We poked amid the still fustiness of the deserted mausoleum behind the castle I knew so well. She thought it odd that the door was unlocked. I said, yes, wasn't it? Then she saw the box, that gleaming copper box which Eve had so thoughtfully provided. She stroked it gently, commenting on its beauty, and before I could prevent it or divert her attention, she had lifted the heavy lid exposing the disarranged shroud, the remains of one or two hapless small creatures with all their blood sucked from them. She screamed and dropped the lid, somehow pinching her finger. She hopped on one foot, as one usually does to fight down sudden pain. Then she was clinging to me, thoroughly frightened.

"What does it mean, Todd?" she pleaded.

I quieted her with the usual platitudes. Then I was kissing that poor, red little finger. Without warning to myself or her, I nipped it affectionately. A warm glow spread through me; there was a taste more delightful than fine old brandy, or vintage wine, and I knew irrevocably that I was not cured; no, nor ever should be! And I knew, too, that I wanted Maria, not just as a man longs for the woman he loves, but to drink of the fountain of her life, that warm, intoxicating fountain, greedily, joyously. She never knew what went through my mind at that moment. If I could have killed myself then, I would have, and with no compunction. But there is more to killing a vampire than that. The church knows the procedure. I hurried Maria home as fast as I could to put her to bed. That night I fought a losing battle with myself, but when she was sleeping I returned to her, partook of her and savoured the life giving force while loathing myself. I knew that I must soon kill the one being I loved above all others, kill, too, her immortal soul, and there was nothing I could do to prevent it. She began to fade visibly. She became during the week you were away so ill that a few steps tired her. Her appetite all but vanished. She was beset by nightmares she said. Could I help her get some rest? I took her to a physician who sagely prescribed a change in climate, rest and a diet rich in blood and iron, gave her a prescription for sedatives, and called it a day. The day was approaching when she would have no more blood, when life as you know it would stop and she would become like me. Somehow I couldn't take her with me without some warning, but I didn't know how to do it since I was an innocent victim myself. I could speak, could warn my intended victim, because although my soul had all but died, there was still a spark that evil had not touched. I knew she would think it a joke if I told her about myself without warning.

For what I have done and what I am asking you to do I ask that you forgive me. I told Maria everything. It was a shock, of course, but she was in love with me, and understood.

I still wonder if she really believed me. We were married three days later. I never told her what her life with me would be like, and that one day I would desert her, fearing and hating her rivalry for the very source of my life. I loved her so. I couldn't betray her then and I can't now.

On the second night of our marriage, she died as you know it, in my arms. We were quite alive when you found us; she was in a hypnotic state induced by her condition. She heard and saw nothing. But I knew. And I must keep my faith. I must, and you are the only one who can help both of us. If you love Maria, you will destroy us. I have told you how.

We rest in the mausoleum during the day in coffins I had specially constructed for us. There you will perform the ancient, effective rites, and you will lay us to rest together, as we wish. That is all I ask. She knows of this request and has signed with me below by a signature you will recognize.

Todd

Maria

When Lon had finished he sat just staring off into space. In substance, Todd, and perhaps even Maria wished him to commit murder. Or how could you commit murder when someone was already dead? He could ignore the request. He could even doubt the veracity of the note. He might be a madman. But he doubted it. He believed every word, and would carry out their wishes out of love for Maria. He would gather all the paraphernalia needed and carry out the task.

That Maria had gone willingly he didn't doubt. He no longer hated Todd so much; rather he pitied him, the hapless victim of a horrible chain of circumstance.

It was seven o'clock in the morning when he approached the mausoleum knowing they had to be back in their resting places before the cock crowed. At night they drew sustenance; during the day they slept.

There were two gleaming copper caskets. Todd had not lied. He approached one warily. In it was nothing but grisly remains, bloodstains and dust. He drew back, fearful. Then he saw the other, newer casket in richest mahogany, almost twice the width of the copper box: Their bridal bed!

They lay together, his arm about her. She wore a gown of palest blue stained with fresh blood. His mouth was dark, rich with blood, slightly open in a half-smile. His hand pressed her fair head close to his chest. She lay trustingly within the circle of his arm, like a small child.

The pit of Lon's stomach was churning madly. He couldn't do it! Not Maria, the lovely woman he loved. But he knew he had to for her sake. She must not wake again to see that blood-stained gown or to wonder at her husband's gory lips. She should know rest, eternal rest. He opened the valise he brought and removed two wooden stakes. Their faces writhed and he felt his skin creep. First he drove a stake into Todd's heart and then into Maria's. The bodies leapt forward in the box, straining against the stake, and a horrible, drawn-out wail shattered the stillness of the tomb. Lon dropped to his knees, and he clapped his hands over his ears, but the dreadful shriek penetrated his soul. His stomach turned over and he retched. Still, he was not through. As the screeching diminished, he removed a hand saw just as the bodies eased back into the coffin. He meticulously severed Todd's head and tossed it into the valise. He then brought the saw gently onto Maria's neck. He couldn't. He had to caress her again before it was done. She lay, small and fragile as ever, her face calm, only there was no trace of life now. She was still and white, and oh so pale, as only the truly dead are. Todd's arm was still flung across her chest, as if to protect her. Lon forced himself to move the arm that belonged to the headless corpse. Then, he stared at his dear Maria as Todd's body slowly disintegrated into a pile of dust that lay piled up around the stake. He could not do it. He could not cut off the head of the woman he loved. Surely, he had done enough.

He walked out of the tomb carrying Todd's head. He found a spot deep in the woods where he piled leaves around it and set it on fire. He walked slowly back to his flat and lay on the bed all day, just staring at the ceiling and thinking of Maria. He fell asleep and did not awaken until the next day. When he did awaken, he felt a slight cut on his neck. He knew then he had to finish the ritual by removing and burning Maria's head for she had come to him from her tomb, come to make him into a creature of the night. He was mortified by

TALES MY GRANDMOTHER TOLD ME

what he had to do, but do it he must, for the sake of the woman he loved.

He went back to the tomb, and to his shock, her coffin was gone. Fearing for his life, he left immediately for Bucharest, where he caught a plane back to North Carolina. For over 50 years now he has sat every night, living with fear few of us will ever know, the fear that there is a beautiful vampire out there coming for him.

J. WAYNE FRYE

Chapter 7
Willie Would Now Rest In Peace

He saw within that valley
What all fear to see,
A form moving fantastically
To a discordant melody,
While like a ghastly rapid river
Through the opening door
A moaning causes a shiver
That frightens to the core.

When I was about 6, my grandmother still did not have indoor plumbing. She would often accompany me to the outhouse, and to my embarrassment, she would sit or stand while watching me use the bathroom, because she feared that my small size might allow me to fall in through the opening into the lime filled pit below. There had many incidents where children had died horrible deaths as a result of this happening.

She used a flashlight to guide our way through the extreme darkness, as we made our way to and from the outhouse, which was about 300 feet from the house. One night, on the way back, in the trees to our right, we saw a thick mist, and within that mist came forth a harrowing, painful, mournful cry, as if someone was suffering immense pain. I said, "Someone is hurt grandmother."

My grandmother replied, "Keep walking Wayne. That is not a living cry."

I did not press the issue, just kept walking with my grandmother. I reached up and took her hand, squeezing it tightly. I always felt safe with her, knowing that she was the light of my life, and I the light of hers.

We got back to the house, and I could not resist asking her, "Do you believe in ghosts?"

Her snuff stained lips parted and she said. "I don't know Wayne, but let me tell you a story. Maybe you can decide then whether I do or do not, or perhaps maybe decide that I am just not sure." Thus began one of her most interesting stories.

My dear great uncle, Raeford Hopkins, in 1892 moved to Asheboro from Denton, where he took up temporary accommodation with his family in a house on Worth Street, until he could find a permanent home for them. It had many advantages which made it peculiarly appropriate. The house is there today, but is not currently lived in, hasn't been for many years.

The old house had the remains of a tower, an indistinguishable old mass of mason-work, overgrown with ivy; and the shells of walls attached to this were half filled up with soil. He had never examined it closely, but there was a large room, or what had been a large room, with the lower part of the windows still existing, on the principal floor, and underneath other windows, which were perfect, though half filled up with fallen soil, and waving with a wild growth of brambles and chance growths of all kinds. At a little distance were some very commonplace and disjointed fragments of the building, one of them suggesting certain pathos by its very commonness and the complete wreck which it showed. There was a huge door on the backside of the tower. Probably it had been a servants' entrance. No offices remained to be entered, pantry and kitchen had all been swept out of being; but there stood the doorway open and vacant, free to all the winds, to the rabbits, and every wild creature. It struck his eye, as a melancholy comment upon a life that was over.

It was when the family had settled down for the winter, when the days were short and dark, and the rigorous reign of frost upon all of Asheboro, that the incidents occurred. These incidents were of so curious a character that he would eventually question their validity. He was absent when these events began. In Charleston, South Carolina he had been circulating among some half-dozen business associates, enjoying their company. He had been so busy that he had failed to read the letters his children had sent. He picked them up and tossed them on the desk each day, but one night, he decided to read them all. He opened several letters, and as was to be expected, the last first, and this was what he read: *"Why don't you come or answer? For God's sake, come. He is much worse."* This was a thunderbolt to fall upon a man's head that had one only son, and he the light of his eyes! The other letter, which he opened with hands trembling so much that he lost time in his haste, was much the same purport: *"No better; doctor afraid of brain-fever. Calls for you day and night. Let nothing detain you."* The first thing he did was to look up the time-tables to see if there was any way of getting off sooner than by the night-train, though he knew well enough there was not; and then he read the other letters, which furnished all the details. They told him that the boy had been pale for some time, with a scared look and that his son, Roland, came home at a wild gallop through the park, his pony panting and in foam, and himself as white as a sheet, with the perspiration streaming from his forehead. For a long time he had resisted all questioning, but at length had developed such strange changes of mood, showing a reluctance to go to school, a desire to be fetched in the carriage at night, which was a ridiculous piece of luxury despite their modest affluence, an unwillingness to go out into the grounds and nervousness at every sound. When the boy, who had never known what fear was, began to talk of voices he had heard in the park, and shadows that had appeared to him among the ruins of the tower, Raeford's wife promptly put him to bed and sent for Dr. Simpson, which, of course, was the only thing to do.

Raeford hurried off that evening, as may be supposed, with an anxious heart. He took the trunk-line from Charlotte to Asheboro, getting in very early in the blackness of the winter morning. He hailed a cabbie and they dashed off to his home. As they passed through the park, he thought he heard some one moaning among the trees. The horses flew like lightning along the intervening path, and drew up at the door all panting, as if they had run a race. Raeford's wife stood waiting to receive him, with a pale face, and a candle in her hand, which made her look paler still as the wind blew the flame about. "He is sleeping," she said in a whisper, as if her voice might wake him. Raeford stood on the steps with her a moment, almost afraid to go in, now that he was there. He grabbed his wife around the waist, and they went up to Roland's room, with not a word between them.

Raeford looked at him from the door of his room, for they were afraid to go near, lest they disturb blessed sleep. It looked like actual sleep, not the lethargy into which Raeford's wife told him he would sometimes fall. She told him everything in the next room. It appeared that ever since the winter began, since it was early dark, and night had fallen before his return from school, he had been hearing voices among the tower ruins near the park by the house, at first only a groaning. The tears ran down Raeford's wife's cheeks as she described to him how he would jump up in the night and cry out, "Oh, mother, let me in! Oh, mother, let me in!" with great pathos. And she, sitting there all the time, only longing to do everything his heart could desire! But though she would try to soothe him, he kept crying those words. She explained how he would often only stare at her, and after a while spring up again with the same cry. At other times he would be quite reasonable, she said, asking eagerly when his father was coming home, but declaring that his father must go with him as soon as he arrived to let them in, but never saying who "they" were that needed to be let in

TALES MY GRANDMOTHER TOLD ME

Perplexed, Raeford replied, "I am at a loss for words, but we will work this out."

The next day there was just daylight enough to see his dear son's face when he went to him; and what a change! He was paler and more worn. His hair seemed to have grown long and lank; his eyes were like blazing lights projecting out of his white face. He got hold of Raeford's hand in a cold and tremulous clutch, and waved to everybody to go away. "Go away, even my mother for I have a secret to share with my father," he said; "go away." This went to her heart, but she left them alone. "Are they all gone?" he said eagerly. "They would not let me speak. The doctor treated me as if I were a fool. You know I am not a fool, papa."

"Yes, my dear boy, I know. But you are ill, and quiet is so necessary. You are not a fool, Roland."

He waved his thin hand with a sort of indignation. "Father, I am not ill," he cried. "Oh, I thought when you came you would not stop me, you would see the sense of it! What do you think is the matter with me, all of you? Dr. Simpson is kind enough; but he is only a doctor. What do you think is the matter with me? I am no more ill than you are. A doctor, of course, he thinks you are ill the moment he looks at you. That's what he's there for, and then it's off to bed with a lot of medicine that rarely does any good, except to put money in the pharmacist's pocket."

"This bed is the best place for you at present, my dear boy."

"I made up my mind," cried the little fellow, "that I would stand it until you came home. I said to myself, I won't frighten mother and the girls. But now, father," he cried, half jumping out of bed, "it's not illness; it's a secret."

His eyes shone so wildly, his face was so swept with strong feeling that Raeford's heart sank within him. He pulled him into his arms. "Roland," he said, "If you are going to tell me this secret to do any good, you know you must be still, and not excite yourself."

"Yes, father," said the boy. He lay back on his pillow, he looked up at Raeford with that grateful, sweet look with which children, when they are ill, break one's heart, the tears coming into his eyes in his weakness. "I was sure as soon as you were here you would know what to do," he said.

"To be sure, my boy. Now keep still and tell it all."

"Yes, father. There is someone in the park, someone that has been badly used, maybe abused."

"Who is this somebody, and who has been ill-using him? We will soon put a stop to that."

"All," cried Roland, "but it is not so easy as you think. I don't know who it is. It is just a cry. Oh, if you could hear it! It gets into my head in my sleep. I heard it so clearly; and they think that I am dreaming or raving perhaps," the boy said.

"Are you quite sure you have not dreamed it, Roland?" Raeford said.

"It is no dream father. It is as real as anything I have ever heard or seen."

O.K., O.K., it is not a dream. Has anyone else heard this voice?"

"The pony heard it, too," he said. "She jumped as if she had been shot. If I had not grasped at the reins, for I was frightened, father......"

"No shame to you, my dear little boy," said Raeford.

"If I hadn't held to her like a leech, she'd have pitched me over her head, and never drew breath till we were at the door. Did the pony dream it?" he said, with a soft disdain. Then he added slowly, "It was only a cry the first time, and all the time before you went away. I wouldn't tell you, for it was so wretched to be frightened. I thought it might be a hare or some other animal, and I went in the morning and looked; but there was nothing. It was after you went I heard it really first; and this is what he said." He raised himself on his elbow close to Raeford, and looked him in the face as he repeated what he had heard 'Oh, mother, let me in! Oh, mother, let me in!' He was pleading, begging." When he said the words a mist came over his face, the mouth quivered, the soft features all melted and changed, and when he had ended these pitiful words, he dissolved into a shower of heavy tears.

"This is very touching, Roland," Raeford said.

His tears now fading, Roland said, "Oh, if you had just heard it, father! My, oh my, it was so pitiful – pitiful beyond words. I said to myself, if father heard it he would do something; but mamma, you know, she's given over to Dr. Simpson for almost any trivial thing, and that fellow's a doctor, and never thinks of anything but clapping you into bed."

"Surely," Raeford said, "No doubt it is some little lost child."

Then he got hold of Raeford's shoulder, clutching it with his thin hand. "Look here," he said, with a quiver in his voice; "suppose it wasn't living at all!"

"My dear boy, how then could you have heard it?" Raeford said.

He turned away from Raeford with a pettish exclamation, "As if you didn't know better than that!"

"Do you want to tell me it is a ghost?" Raeford said.

Roland withdrew his hand; his countenance assumed an aspect of great dignity and gravity; a slight quiver remained about his lips. "Whatever it was does not matter. It was something in trouble. Oh, father, in terrible trouble!"

"But, my boy, if it was a child that was lost, or any poor human creature, what is it you want me to do?"

"I depend on you for answers papa. I have had to face it night after night, in such terrible, terrible trouble, and never to be able to do it any good! I don't want to cry; it's like a baby, I know; but what else can I do? Out there all by itself in the ruin, and nobody to help it! I can't bear it! I can't bear it!"

Raeford was perplexed finding his child's mind possessed with the conviction that he had seen, or heard, a ghost; but that he should require him to help that ghost was the most bewildering experience that had ever come his way. Of course,

Raeford did not believe in ghosts, but still he did his best to console Roland without giving any promise of going ghost hunting.

His voice quivering, Roland said, "It will be there, father. It will be there all the night! Oh, think, papa, think if it was me! I can't rest for thinking of it. You go and help it, and mother can take care of me."

"But, Roland, what can I do?"

"You will know what to do?"

Such confidence he had in his father. How could he deny the boy? So, he called his wife to take care of him, as he said that to his wife that he had to take care of a problem.

The girls were astonished at the ease with which their father was taking it. "How do you think he is?" they said in a breath, coming round him?

"Not half so ill as I expected," he said; "not very bad at all."

"Oh, papa, you are a darling!" cried Agatha, kissing him, and crying upon his shoulder; while little Jeanie, who was as pale as Roland, clasped both her arms around him, and was so concerned she could not speak at all.

He left them to act the part of a father to Roland's ghost, which made him almost laugh, though he might just as well have cried.

He walked past the ruins of the tower into the heart of the shrubberies two or three times, not seeing a step before him, until he came out upon the broader carriage-road, where the trees opened a little, and there was a faint gray glimmer of sky visible, under which the great elms stood darkling like ghosts; but it grew black again as he approached the corner where the ruins lay. Both eyes and ears were on the alert, as may be supposed; but he could see nothing in the absolute gloom and heard nothing. Nevertheless, there came a strong impression upon him that somebody was there. He called out sharply, "Who's there?" Nobody answered, nor did he expect any one to answer. He walked briskly toward a nearby cottage where the property caretaker lived, a man named Jarvis.

Jarvis and his wife invited him in, and Raeford said before he even sat down, "Do you know anything about strange noises in the woods by the tower ruins?"

"Oh sir," Jarvis said, as he looked quizzically over at his wife who was sitting by the fireplace knitting, "There have been tales of voices in those woods. It is a haunted place, no doubt." It became obvious that in the opinion of the Jarvis family the place was haunted beyond all doubt. As Jarvis and his wife warmed to the tale, one tripping up another in their eagerness to tell everything, it gradually developed as distinct a superstition as Raeford had ever heard, and not without poetry and pathos. How long it was since the voice had been heard first, nobody could tell with certainty. Jarvis' opinion was that his father, who had been coachman at the property before him, had never heard anything about it, and that the whole thing had arisen within the last ten years, since complete crumbling of the old tower. According to witnesses, and to several whom Raeford questioned afterwards, and who were all in perfect agreement, it was only in the months of November and December that "the visitation" occurred. During these months, the darkest of the year, scarcely a night passed without the recurrence of these inexplicable cries. Nothing, it was said, had ever been seen, at least, nothing that could be identified. Some people, bolder or more imaginative than the others, had seen the darkness moving, Mrs. Jarvis said. It began when night fell, and continued, at intervals, until day broke. Very often it was only inarticulate cries and moaning, but sometimes the words were distinctly audible, "Oh, mother, let me in!" Jarvis and his wife were not aware that there had ever been any investigation into it. Many had rented the place but few had remained after December.

Anger actually grew within Raeford toward the owners from whom he had rented the place, as if he had been warned he might have taken precautions, or avoided the place.

Raeford's curiosity was intense to solve this dilemma but everything in him seemed to cry out against it. His heart thumped, beating against his ears. It was very dark; as he left the Jarvis pair to tread about the accursed tower by the woods. Suddenly, his foot strayed out of the path in his confusion and he felt himself knock against something solid. What was it? The blood was chilled in his veins, a shiver stole along his spine and his faculties seemed to forsake him. Close by, at his side, at his feet, there was a sigh, a perfectly soft, faint, inarticulate sigh. He sprang back, and his heart seemed to stop beating. He was mesmerized by the sound of a long, soft, weary sigh, as if drawn to the utmost, and emptying out a load of sadness that filled the breast. He felt something cold creeping over him, up into his hair and down to the feet, which refused to move. He cried out, with a trembling voice, "Who is there?" as he had done before; but there was no reply.

He got home, and in his mind there was no longer any indifference as to the thing, whatever it was, that haunted these ruins. His scepticism disappeared like a mist.

Raeford had made one good friend in the brief time he had been in Asheboro. Bobby Borstal was summoned the next evening, and Raeford informed him of all that had occurred. A sceptical Bobby said he would go with Raeford that night to the area where he had heard the crying.

It was ten o'clock when they set out. All was perfectly quiet indoors. Raeford's wife, Lil, was with Roland, who had been quite calm, and who (though, no doubt, the fever must run its course) had been better ever since his dad came home.

Raeford told Bobby to put on a thick coat that he lent him over his evening coat, and did the same himself, with strong boots; for the soil was like a sponge or worse. Talking to him, he almost forgot what they were going to do. It was darker even than it had been before, and Bobby kept very close to him as they went along. He had a small lantern in his hand, which gave adequate guidance. They had come to the corner where the path turned. On one side was an area which the girls had taken possession of for a croquet-ground, a wonderful enclosure surrounded by high hedges of holly, and on the other side, the ruins of the tower. Both were bleakly black; but before they got very far, there was a little opening in which they could just discern the trees and the lighter line of the road. He thought it best to pause there and take a breath. "Bobby," he said, "There is something about these ruins I don't understand. It is over there I am going. Keep your eyes open and your wits about you. Are you game to follow me, my man?"

Bobby nodded affirmatively and they proceeded on their way. Within a few seconds, they heard that sigh. The darkness, however, was so complete that all marks, as of trees or paths, disappeared. One moment they felt their feet on the gravel, another sinking noiselessly into the slippery grass. Raeford had shut off his lantern, not wishing to scare anyone or anything. Bobby followed exactly in his footsteps towards the mass of the ruined tower. After a while they stood still to see, or rather feel, where they were. The darkness was very still, but no stiller than is usual in a winter's night. As they stood still there came up from the trees the prolonged hoot of an owl. Bobby was startled with alarm, being in a state of general nervousness.

"An owl," Raeford said, in a whisper.

All at once, quite suddenly, close to them, at their feet, broke out a cry. Raeford made a spring backwards in the first moment of surprise and horror and in doing so came sharply against rough masonry and brambles, as this new sound came upwards from the ground, a low, moaning, wailing voice, full of suffering and pain. The contrast between it and the hoot of the owl was describable, the one with a wholesome wildness and naturalness that hurt nobody; the other, a sound that made one's blood curdle, full of human misery. Raeford slid his lantern back on. The light leapt out like something living, and made the place visible in a moment. They were inside the ruined building. The light showed a bit of wall, the ivy glistening upon it in clouds of dark green, the bramble-branches waving, and below, an opened dilapidated door, a door that led to nothing. It was from this the voice came which died out just as the light flashed upon this strange scene. There was a moment's silence, and then it broke forth again. The sound was so near, so penetrating, so pitiful, that, in the nervous start he gave, the light fell out of his hand. As he groped for it in the dark his hand was clutched by Bobby, who, had dropped upon his knees. He clutched at Raeford in the confusion of his terror. "For God's sake, what is it?" he gasped.

A perplexed Raeford, replied, "I can't tell any more than you; that's what we've got to find out. Up, man, up!" He pulled him to his feet. "Will you go round and examine the other side, or will you stay here with the lantern?"

Bobby gasped at him with a face of horror. "Can't we stay together?" he said as his knees were trembling under him.

Raeford pushed him against the corner of a wall, and put the light into his hands. "Stand fast till I come back; shake yourself together, man; let nothing pass you," he said.

Raeford went to the other side of the crumbled wall, keeping close to it. The light shook in Bobby's hand, but, tremulous though it was, shining out through all the holes in the wall, one oblong block of light marked all the crumbling corners and hanging masses of foliage. Suddenly, Bobby flew at Raeford, gripping his shoulder. But at that moment the voice burst forth again between them, at their feet. Bobby, in shock, dropped off from Raeford, and fell against the wall, his jaw dropping with terror. Raeford snatched the light out of his hand, and flashed it all about wildly. Nothing could be seen, but something could still be heard – the crying. It was close to their ears now, crying, crying, pleading as if for life. The voice went on, growing into distinct articulation, but wavering about, now from one point, now from another, as if the owner of it were moving slowly back and forward. "Mother! Mother!" and then an outburst of wailing. As Raeford's mind steadied, getting accustomed (as one's mind gets accustomed to anything), it seemed to him as if some uneasy, miserable creature was pacing up and down near them. He thought he heard a sound like knocking, and then another burst of pleading, "Oh, mother! Mother!"

"Do you hear it, Bobby? Do you hear what it is saying?" But Bobby was lying against the wall, his eyes glazed, half dead with terror. He made a motion of his lips as if to answer Raeford, but no sounds came; then he lifted his hand with a curious imperative movement as if ordering Raeford to be silent and listen as the voice kept saying "Oh, mother, let me in! Oh, mother, mother, let me in! Oh, let me in!"

Every word was clear. At last the words died away, and there was a sound of sobs and moaning. Raeford cried out, "Who are you?" There was no answer; the moaning went on, and then, as if it had been real, the voice rose a little higher again, the words recommenced, "Oh, mother, let me in! Oh, mother, let me in!" with an expression that was heart-breaking to hear.

Raeford had forgotten Bobby, who had almost fainted in terror. He was leaning against the wall. Raeford helped him get settled on his feet, and led him to the house as best he could, making him lean upon his arm. The great fellow was as weak as a child.

"You've got an epidemic in your house," Dr. Simpson said to Raeford the next morning. "What's the meaning of it all? Here's your friend raving about a voice in the darkness, and you apparently believe in this poppycock, too."

"Yes, I do, doctor. I thought I had better speak to you. Of course you are treating Roland all right, but the boy is not raving, he is as sane as you or I are. It's all true."

"As sane as I or you? I never thought the boy insane." The doctor shrugged his shoulders, but he listened to Raeford patiently. He did not believe a word of the story he was told. That was clear, but he heard it all from beginning to end. "My dear fellow," he said, "the boy told me just the same.

It's mass hysteria. When one person falls a victim to this sort of thing, it's as safe as can be, there's always two or three."

"Then how do you account for it?" Raeford said.

"Oh, account for it? That's a different matter; there's often no accounting for many psychological manifestations created in the brain. It may be delusion, some trick of the echoes or the winds, some phonetic disturbance or some other phenomena, but believe me it is not a ghost."

"Come with me tonight, and judge for yourself," Raeford said.

Upon this Simpson laughed aloud and then said, "That's not such a bad idea; but it would ruin me forever if it were known that Doctor Simpson was ghost-hunting."

"There it is," said Raeford; "you are a scientific man, but do not blot out the unscientific, because some things deny scientific explanation. If you prove it to be a delusion, I shall be very happy to apologize for wasting your time."

It was agreed that Raeford should meet him at the gate, and that they should visit the scene of the occurrences. The day seemed to Raeford a very long one, as he had to spend a certain part of it with Roland, which was a terrible ordeal for him, for what could he say to the boy? The improvement continued, but he was still in a very precarious state, and the trembling vehemence with which he turned to his father when his mother left the room filled Raeford with alarm.

"Father?" he said quietly' "tell me of what you are doing to assess the situation at the tower."

Raeford replied, "I am giving my best attention to it; all is being done that I can do. I have not come to any conclusion, yet. I am neglecting nothing you said, though."

What he could not do was to give the boy's inquisitive mind any encouragement to dwell upon the mystery. It was a hard predicament, for some satisfaction had to be given him. He looked at Raeford very wistfully, with the great blue eyes which shone so large and brilliant out of his white and worn face as his father said, "You must trust me."

"I do."

That night at eleven he met Doctor Simpson at the gate. Raeford had his lantern and he said to him, "There is nothing like light."

It was a very still night, scarcely a sound, but not so dark. Raeford led him to the spot where he and Bobby had stood on the previous night. All was silent as a winter night could be, so silent that they heard far off the sound of the horses in the stables, the shutting of a window at a nearby house. Simpson had brought his own lantern and held it high as he poked into all the corners. They looked like two conspirators lying in wait for some unfortunate traveller; but not a sound broke the quiet. A star or two shone over them in the sky, looking down as if surprised at the strange proceedings. Simpson did nothing but utter subdued laughs under his breath. "I thought as much," he said. "It is just the same with tables and all other kinds of ghostly apparatus; a sceptic's presence stops everything. When I am present nothing ever comes off. How long do you think it will be necessary to stay here?"

"It seems, indeed," Raeford said, "that there is to be no manifestation tonight."

Suddenly, a moan could be heard. It started from some distance off, and came towards them, nearer and nearer, like someone walking along and moaning to himself. The approach was slow, like that of a weak person, with little halts and pauses. They heard it coming along the grass straight towards the tower doorway. Simpson had been a little startled by the first sound. He said hastily, "That child has no business to be out so late." But he felt, Raeford could tell, that this was no child's voice. As it came nearer, Simpson grew silent, and, going to the doorway with his lantern, stood looking out towards the sound. If he was afraid, he concealed it with great success, but he was perplexed. And then all that had happened on the previous night was enacted once more. Every cry, every sob seemed the same as before.

Raeford listened almost without any emotion at all, thinking of its effect upon Simpson. He maintained a very bold front, on the whole. All that coming and going of the voice was, if his ears could be trusted, exactly in front of the doorway, blazing full of light, which caught and shone in the glistening leaves of the great hollies at a little distance. Not a rabbit could have crossed the turf without being seen; but there was nothing. After a time, Simpson, with a certain caution and bodily reluctance, went toward the sounds. Just at this moment the voice sank, as was its custom, and seemed to fling itself down at the doorway. Simpson recoiled violently, as if someone had come up against him, then turned, and held his lantern low, as if examining something. "Do you see anybody?" Raeford cried in a whisper, feeling the chill of nervous panic steal over him.

Simpson was scoffing no longer; his face was contracted and pale. "How long does this go on?" he whispered to Raeford.

"It will stop soon," replied Raeford, and it did.

They walked home very silent afterwards. It was only when they were in sight of the house that Raeford said, "What do you think of it?"

"I can't tell what to think of it," Simpson replied quickly. They went into the house and Simpson was handed a glass of brandy. "Mind you, I don't believe a word of it," he said after taking a sip.

All of this did Raeford no good with the solution of the perplexing problem he faced. If he was to help this weeping, sobbing thing, which was already to him a distinct personality, what was he to do? What really troubled him was what to say to poor Roland, who longed to help this thing. He did not know if it was man or woman or some other entity; but he no longer doubted that it was a soul in pain, and it was his business now to soothe that pain partly because his dear boy shared the entity's pain. He had to ease his own son's pain by helping it. He simply had no other choice.

Next morning Simpson was there before breakfast, and came in with evident signs of the damp grass on his boots, and a look of worry and weariness, which did not say much for the night he experienced. He improved a little after breakfast, and visited his patient, who was still an invalid reeling from worry about the voice. Upon leaving, Simpson stood in the doorway and said, "Your son is doing well as there are no complications. But mind you, that's not a boy to be trifled with. Not a word to him about last night."

Raeford had to tell him then of his last interview with Roland, and of the impossible demand he had made upon him. Doctor Simpson said very determinedly, "We must just perjure ourselves all round and swear you exorcised it. It's frightfully serious for your son. I wish I saw a way out of it, for your sake. By the way," he added shortly, "didn't you notice that juniper bush on the left-hand side of the door?"

"Yes. So what?"

"I walked back there this morning. There's no juniper, left or right. Just go and see." He turned and walked away, then stopped and looked back at Raeford and said, "I'm coming back tonight. Maybe that was not a bush we saw."

Just as Simpson was leaving, up the walkway came the neighbour, Hap Lawson. "Morning Mr. Hopkins, just dropped by to ask if you have noticed strange lights in and around that old Tower, near the park.

For a second he wondered whether he should tell the truth or not, and then he decided that the truth might elicit some useful response from his neighbour. He told him the story, more than he had told Simpson. The old man listened with keen interest.

"Your son is a good soul," offered Lawson. "God bless the boy! I have observed him often. There's something more than common in him, and also the faith of him in his father." Then the old gentleman gave Raeford an alarmed look, and said, "I think I'll come tonight if it is O.K. I'm an old man. I'm less liable to be frightened than those that are further off from death."

"Please, you are welcome. Come tonight at 11:00."

Lawson left after giving Raeford a pat on the shoulder, and assuring him all would be alright. Raeford had his doubts. He had no doubt that what was out there was not an illusion. He was 100% sure of its existence. To hear it first was a great shock to his nerves, but not now, as a man will get accustomed to anything. But to do something for it was the great problem. How was he to be serviceable to a being that was invisible, that was mortal no longer?

He went for his morning walk and invariably he wound up by the tower and nearby park. There was full sunshine. The ruined tower looked due east, and in the present aspect of the sun the light streamed down through the doorway, throwing a flood of light upon the damp grass beyond. There was a strange suggestion in the open door, so futile, a kind of emblem of vanity, so that you could go where you pleased, and yet that semblance of an enclosure, that way of entrance, unnecessary, leading to nothing. And why any creature should pray and weep to get in to nothing, or be kept out by nothing. He could not dwell upon it, or it might make his brain ache. He remembered, however, what Simpson said about the juniper, with a little smile on his own mind as to the inaccuracy of recollection which even a scientific man will be guilty of. He remembered the light of his lantern gleaming upon the wet glistening surface of the spiky leaves at the right hand of the doorway. He went round to make sure there was no juniper. And then he saw what he had said. Right or left there was no juniper at all! He was confounded by this, though it was entirely a matter of detail, a bush of brambles waving, the grass growing up to the very walls. But after all, though it gave him a shock for a moment, what did that matter? There were marks as if a number of footsteps had been up and down in front of the door, but these might have been his, Bobby's and Simpson's steps. All was bright and peaceful and still. He poked about the ruin. There were marks upon the grass here and there, but that told for nothing one way or another. He examined the ruined rooms closely. They were half filled up with soil and debris. Discouraged, he headed back to the main house. He avoided going to see Roland, because he had no answers for the boy's concerns.

Simpson came to dinner, and when the house was all still, and the servants in bed, they waited for Lawson. His knock on the door reverberated through the house like the knock on a tomb door signalling the dead to rise.

"One thing is certain, you know; there must be some human agency," Simpson said.

All three had lanterns. They had a rapid consultation as they went up, and the result was that they divided to different posts. Simpson remained inside the wall, if you can call that inside where there was no wall but one. Lawson placed himself on the side next to the ruins, so as to intercept any communication, which was what his mind was fixed upon for an unknown reason. Raeford was posted on the far side. To say that nothing could come near without being seen was self-evident. It had been so also on the previous night. Now, with their three lights in the midst of the darkness, the whole place seemed illuminated. Doctor Simpson's lantern, which was a large one, an old-fashioned lantern with a pierced and ornamental top, shone steadily, the rays shooting out of it upward into the gloom. He placed it on the grass, where the middle of the room, if this had been a room, would have been. The usual effect of the light streaming out of the doorway was prevented by the illumination of Lawson's lantern and Raeford's on either side. With these differences, no one was surprised or alarmed when they heard the moaning and crying which seized their hearts with pity, pity for the poor suffering creature that moaned and pleaded so. However, it was Lawson who seemed most affected.

They were all perfectly still until the first outburst was exhausted. But just as it threw itself sobbing at the door, there suddenly came a voice, Lawson's voice. It came out with a sort of stammering, as if too much moved for utterance. "Willie, Willie! Oh, God preserve us! Is it you?"

Raeford thought the old man had gone mad with terror. He made a dash around to the other side of the wall, half crazed with concern for Lawson. He was standing where he had left him, his shadow thrown vague and large upon the grass by the lantern which stood at his feet. He lifted his own light to see his face as he rushed forward. He was very pale, his eyes wet and glistening, his mouth quivering with parted lips. He neither saw nor heard Raeford. They that had gone through this experience before had crouched towards each other to get a little strength to bear it. But he was not even aware that they were there as his whole being seemed absorbed in anxiety and tenderness. He held out his hands, which trembled, but it seemed to Simpson and Raeford to be with eagerness, not fear. He went on speaking all the time. "Willie, if it is you, if it is not an illusion why come you here freighting them that know you not? Why come you not to me?"

He seemed to wait for an answer. When his voice ceased, his countenance, every line moving, continued to speak. Simpson gave Raeford another terrible shock, stealing into the open doorway with his light, awe stricken, wildly curious. But then Lawson resumed, without seeing Simpson. "Is this right to come here? Your mother's gone with your name on her lips. Do you think she would ever close her door on her own lad? No!"

The sobbing voice had begun to resume its cries. Lawson made a step forward, calling out the last words in a voice of command. "I forbid you! Cry out no more to anyone. Go home, you wandering spirit! Go home! Do you hear me? Me, who was at your christening." Here the loud tones of his voice sank into tenderness. "And her too, poor woman! Poor woman! Her you are calling upon. She's not here. You'll find her in eternity. Go there and seek her, not here. Do you hear me, lad? Go after her there. She'll let you in, though it's late. Man, take heart! If you will lie and sob and greet, let it be at eternity's gate, and not your poor mother's ruined door. She died crying for you. Be gone spirit!"

He stopped to get his breath; and the voice had stopped, not as it had done before, when its time was exhausted and all its repetitions said, but with a sobbing catch in the breath as if overruled. Then Lawson spoke again, "Are you hearing me, Will? Oh, laddie. Be gone. Be gone. Are you hearing me?" Then, the old man sank down upon his knees, his face raised upwards, his hands held up with a tremble in them, all white in the light in the midst of the darkness. Raeford resisted as long as he could, then he, too, dropped upon his knees.

Simpson all the time stood in the doorway, with an expression on his face such as words could not tell, his under lip dropped, his eyes wild, staring. All the time the voice, with a low arrested sobbing, emanating from just where he was standing.

Raeford leaped up and sprang forward to catch a transparent mist that was undulating in the doorway. It looked like a bush! He plunged right though it, not pausing until he felt his forehead graze against the wall and his hands clutch the ground, for there was nobody there to grasp.

TALES MY GRANDMOTHER TOLD ME

Simpson held out his hand to help him up. He was trembling and cold, his lower lip hanging, his speech almost inarticulate. "It's gone," he said, stammering, "It's gone!" They leaned upon each other for a moment, trembling so much, both of them, that the whole scene trembled as if it were going to dissolve and disappear.

Through it all was the kneeling figure with all the whiteness of the light concentrated on his white venerable head and uplifted hands. A strange solemn stillness seemed to close all round them. Lawson was mumbling, "Willie, Willie." At last he rose from his knees, and standing up at his full height, raised his arms toward the heavens and said, "If you are indeed real and up there God, please take this poor soul into your arms."

Simpson and Raeford took the shaken Lawson by his arms and led him back toward the house. No words were spoken between them.

It was as if they were coming from a deathbed. Something hushed and solemnized the very air. There was that sense of relief in it which there always is at the end of a death struggle. And nature, persistent, never daunted, came back in all of them, as they returned into the ways of life. The silence continued for a time; but when they got clear of the trees and reached the opening near the house, Lawson said, "Do either of you believe in purgatory, a place or state of suffering inhabited by the souls of sinners who are expiating their sins before going to heaven

"Sir," said Doctor Simpson, "a man like me is sometimes not very sure what he believes. There is just one thing I am certain of, and that is what I experienced tonight was no illusion. Tell us though. How did you know that thing, that voice?"

"Sir," said the old man again, with a tremor in him, "if I saw a friend of mine within the gates of hell, I would not despair but rather take his hand to console him."

"Yes," offered Raeford, I understand that, but you knew the voice."

"How should I not recognize a person that I know better, far better, than I know either of you?"

Simpson asked, "We did not see him. Did you?"

Lawson made no reply, but moved along, turning toward his own house without another word, threading the dark paths, which were steep and slippery with the damp of the winter. The air was very still, not more than enough to make a faint sighing in the branches, which mingled with the chirping of crickets.

Raeford and Doctor Simpson stood looking at each other, wondering what Lawson was hiding. Who was the person, the voice that Lawson recognized so well?

The sky was clearer than it had been for many nights, with a full moon shining high over the trees, with here and there a star faintly gleaming through the wilderness of dark and bare branches. The air was very soft on them, with a subdued and peaceful cadence. It was real, like every natural sound, and came to them like a hush of peace and relief. They thought there was a sound in it, a sort of whisper.

Suddenly, Lawson appeared again, having turned and walked back. He had a forlorn look as he said, "I apologize, but I was so dumbfounded, so distraught to hear Willie's voice. He was someone who was a lost child from almost the very beginning. He had been a prodigal, weak, foolish, easily imposed upon and led astray, as people say. Of course, that did not excuse those who took advantage of him. He had been abused by a clergyman, and apparently by some other prominent well-known citizen. This came out after he left town. The clergyman also left town never to be heard from again, and the prominent citizen, well, no one ever discovered who that was. Maybe it was just a rumour, but I believe it, believe that there are those in our midst who are demons, sick individuals who have no control over their carnal urges. Oh, this man, if it did happen, is an abomination. He should do the world a favour and end his own life if necessary to rid the world of his evil. He did not only destroy the young boy's life, but his mother's life as well. The young man fled town when the truth was discovered, fled town in shame, as if it was he who was at fault, a lad of only fourteen years of age. His mother pined for him while she grieved over how his life was ruined by the evil of two men, maybe more. He came home after being gone a year, but his mother had died two days before. He was so distraught, so pained when he heard of her death that he threw himself down at the door and called upon her to let him in." The old man could scarcely speak of it through his cascading tears.

"And what of Willie; what happened to him," asked Raeford.

The tears continued, as he said, "That boy crying on the steps for his mother, who was a housekeeper in the main house and lived in the tower lower rooms, that poor abused boy took out a pocket knife and slit his wrists at only fifteen years of age. Dying, as the life force flowed from him, staining the ground with his blood. He lay in front of the door still pleading for his mother to let him in. The uncaring people in the main house just ignored his cries and went off to bed. I heard them, too, but to my dying shame, I also ignored them, assuming he would eventually realize that his mother would never answer that door again. Thus ends the painful story, but perhaps it has not ended at all, perhaps there is one more death that is required to atone for the evil perpetrated on poor Willie."

"The prominent man who abused him," said Simpson.

"Yes," replied Lawson, as he turned and walked back toward his house with stooped shoulders.

To Raeford it seemed as if the world was far too filled with pain. Seeing that old man walk away made him realize that the world is also filled with evil. No doubt, that old man would go to his grave carrying the guilt of not answering the cries of a dying boy.

Another thing that struck him was how near Roland was to Willie's age. His poor son's pain for that poor entity, or whatever it was, in its misery, made him realize how truly precious his son was. He bade the doctor good night and rushed to the house to share the story of what happened with Roland.

Roland spoke to him quietly. "Father, then you were unable to help the thing, help it deal with the pain? I am still troubled."

"There is some pain that cannot be assuaged. I shall walk by there again late at night tomorrow to see if the voices of pain can still be heard."

Smiling, Roland said, "It is O.K. father. And I am O.K. regardless; because I know that my loving father has done all he could." He reached up and pulled his father to him in a loving embrace.

Their tender moment was interrupted by a single gunshot in the distance. They passed it off as someone firing a gun in the nearby woods. That night, he walked by the old tower consistently, but not a sound did he hear. Was the spirit finally at rest?

He peeped though the underbrush and saw a horse drawn ambulance and several police wagons at Lawson's home. Curious, he wondered over, but was stopped by a constable from getting closer to the house. He said to the constable, "What has happened?"

The constable replied, "The former mayor, Hap Lawson, committed suicide this afternoon, apparently."

A wave of disbelief swept over Raeford. You could not get more prominent in a small town than being mayor. Yes, Willie would now rest in peace.

TALES MY GRANDMOTHER TOLD ME

Chapter 9
The Naked Truth

I am the truth
I am the ancient phoenix.
I rise defiantly toward the sun,
Spreading my wings in glory.

The heat might turn me to ashes,
And those ashes may fall to earth.
Oh, but I shall rise again,
For I am resilient and determined.

I might be knocked down,
But I am never defeated
Just because the lie is embraced by those
Who do not seek truth.

Those people live in the darkness
To absorbed in hatred to search for facts.
They are the lost souls who
Cannot face the naked truth!

In 2016, a man used lies and deceit to fool people into believing he could be their saviour. Truth became a casualty in the process, as he piled lie upon lie to make the disenchanted believe his lies were truth. He ridiculed anybody that dared call out those lies. He was not only corrupt to his very core, having no moral compass whatsoever, but he was so masterful at appealing to the disenchanted with his misogyny, his racism, his blind self-aggrandisement that the people, so

J. WAYNE FRYE   189

thoroughly brainwashed, actually lined up for the balls and chains he was offering them. My grandmother had been dead almost fifty years when he was elected President of the United States. However, in 1967, she told me a story that seems terribly prophetic. I often wonder if in her infinite wisdom way back then that she actually saw the coming of a great charlatan like Donald Trump, whose lack of character and reckless disregard for the truth would bring fatal moral decay to a nation that had already been on a long moral decline. I share that story herein, because it illustrates the ease with which the truth can be snuffed out by lies.

She rocked back and forth by the seldom used fireplace and said, "Wayne, you know how I have always insisted you be truthful. You also know the consequences when you have not been truthful. You recall the incident with your cousin Monte about the wooden well?"

"I do grandmother. I do, and I am still ashamed for my deceitfulness."

I will digress a bit here, as in order to understand how easy it is to manipulate people, and to comprehend the depth of the message within my grandmother's story about truth, I believe it necessary to relate the story of *Wayne, Monte and the Old Well*.

Now, my cousin Monte was four years younger than I, and he, for some unknown reason, adored me. He was also very naïve. Being someone who was called a marketing genius by the Los Angeles Times in 1992, perhaps even at ten I was already practicing the trade I called "the manipulative art," when I taught MBA students majoring in marketing, or when I was President of two universities that grew in student numbers rapidly under my tutelage, or when I was a hockey coach who dabbled in promotion to fill the arena night after night. My point being, that I understand marketing, because I not only got a Ph.D. in it, but more importantly, studied it under the master marketer, Worth Frye, my father. That is why I firmly believe the banal tripe we see on television today is not meant to entertain. It is simply meant to soften up the brain cells so corporations can convince people that happiness must be bought. The commercials do not interrupt the programs. It is the programs that interrupt the commercials. That is why I got rid of television in 2009, because I grew weary of watching ridiculous programs that needed an intrusive laugh track to make people laugh, because the shows were not funny enough to do so without it. People must be brainwashed into believing something is funny. In other words, almost everything boils down to marketing, and the more naïve a person is, the easier it is to manipulate and control them, as evidenced by the aforementioned Donald Trump, and also by my six year old cousin way back "in the day."

Monte and I loved playing with a small old wooden well my grandmother had setting on her coffee table. Her father had carved it for her way back at the turn of the 20th century. I once asked her if I could put water in it. She adamantly said, "No, it will crack it and ruin the well."

TALES MY GRANDMOTHER TOLD ME

Still, I wanted to see for myself if it would crack. I didn't believe it would. Of course, I did not want to get in trouble, so when my grandmother went out of the room, I whispered to Monte, "Wouldn't you like to see water in the well. It would be more fun to play with. We could draw water out of it and dink it out of a cup. That would be so much fun."

Monte, ever easy to manipulate, replied, "Sure. You think it is O.K., Wayne."

"Of course it is Monte," I said with a bit of excitement in my voice just to make sure he was excited about the proposition also.

He went to the kitchen, got a cup of water, returned, and with my encouragement, he poured the water into the well. It immediately began to crack and water ran out the sides, just as my grandmother walked in.

She was appalled at what she saw, and before she even asked, I pointed at naïve Monte and said, "He did it."

She gave me a stern look and said, "He may have done it, Wayne, but you are the one who manipulated him into doing it, so you are the one who will be punished. You do not get away with lies in this house."

To this very day, that incident resonates with me, because my grandmother was smart enough to see through my lie. I had convinced Monte to do it, but I was more the culprit than he was, because I was older and should not have taken advantage of someone who was naïve. So now, let us look at the story I have always called "The Naked Truth."

TALES MY GRANDMOTHER TOLD ME

My grandmother was rocking incessantly as she told the story. In fact, I could see, as I often did that this would be a story that would stay with me for many years, because when she rocked harder than usual, I knew that there would be great profundity in the moral she was trying to teach me.

According to a 19th century legend, the Truth and the Lie meet one summer day when the sun is out and there is a cool breeze blowing. It is a beautiful day, and all seems right with the world.

The Lie says to the Truth: "It's a marvellous day." The Truth looks up to the skies and sighs, for the day was really beautiful. They spend a lot of time together, just walking about and enjoying the cool breeze, ultimately arriving beside a soaking well.

The Lie tells the Truth: "The water is very nice, let's take a bath together!"

The Truth is suspicious of Lie's motives, but tests the water and discovers that it indeed is very nice. They undress and start bathing. Suddenly, the Lie comes out of the water, puts on the clothes of the Truth and runs away, carrying his own clothes.

The furious Truth comes out of the well and runs everywhere to find the Lie and to get her clothes back. The World, seeing the Truth naked, turns its gaze away, with contempt and rage.

The poor Truth returns to the well and disappears, hiding therein its shame. Since then, the Lie travels around the world, dressed as the Truth, satisfying the needs of society, because the world harbours no wish at all to meet the naked Truth."

TALES MY GRANDMOTHER TOLD ME
Epilogue
The Bonds of Love

She was a spinner of tales,
A weaver of joy and horror.
The tales were given her as presents,
And then they became gifts to me.

A story well-told could make me
Laugh, cry or scream with fear.
Some gave me strength and courage,
For there was wit, beauty and charm.

She is long gone now,
But her stories live on within me.
She is immortal for that reason,
As her stories continue season after season.

Oral storytelling is an ancient art form that has largely disappeared today as a result of the impersonalization of modern society. My grandmother was a master storyteller, and I practiced the art in a way as a university professor, because I found that relating stories to illustrate what my students read in a book was a great way to bring a subject to life.

As a storyteller, my grandmother was not just physically close to me, but was able to reach my inner self, able to transcend time and space in a way that elevated our relationship. Through the telling of a story, we became psychologically close, developing a connection to one another through the communal experience. The intimacy and connection was deepened by the flexibility of her storytelling which allowed the tale to be moulded according to my needs at any given time. As a listener, I experienced the urgency of the creative process taking place and embraced the empowerment of being a part of that creative process. Her storytelling created a personal bond that has continued long after her death. A thousand years from now, ten thousand years from now, those stories will live on as long as grandmother and grandchild share the bonds of love.

TALES MY GRANDMOTHER TOLD ME

<u>**Some of the books by J. Wayne Frye**</u>
For Young People
Lynton Curls Her Hair
Lynton Walks on Water
Lynton and the Vampire at Tagaytay Manor
Lynton Buys a Cell-Phone and Hears the Voice of Doom
Lynton Viñas and Beowulf Perez in the Taal Inferno
Lynton and the Ghosts in the Mansion on Balete Drive
Lynton Viñas: Shadow in the Darkness
Lynton's South African Adventure
Lynton, the Karoo Vampire and the Jewels of Omar Bin Abi
Lynton and the Stellenbosch Terror
Lynton and the Cape Town Ghost
Lynton and the Haunting of the HMS Wind Dancer
Hockey Mania and the Mystery of Nancy Running Elk
White Meteors and the Ghost of Sue Ann McGee
How Hockey Saved a Jew From the Holocaust
Sammy Sasquatch and the Sts'ailes Star

For Adults
Something Evil in the Darkness at Hopkins House
The Girl Who Said Goodbye for the Last Time
The Girl Who Motivated Murder Most Foul
The Girl Who Stirred up the Whirlwind
The Girl Who Rode into a Storm
Fall From Apocalypse
Armageddon Now
Worth Part 1: Roaring Through Life Like a Comet
in the Midnight Sky
Worth Part 2: The Night of Thunder Road
When Jesus Came to Jersey as the Son of Thunder
When Jesus Came to Canada to Lead an Indigenous
Rebellion
When Jesus Came to the Black Hills to do the Ghost Dance
Chablis: Avenging Angel for the Forgotten
Chablis and the Terrorist
Pursuit
The Disappearance
The Rectifier: Dance of Death in the Darkness of Retribution

TALES MY GRANDMOTHER TOLD ME

Other exciting ghost stories from
J. Wayne Frye

TALES MY GRANDMOTHER TOLD ME

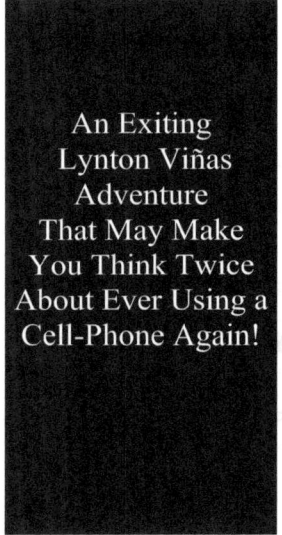

An Exiting
Lynton Viñas
Adventure
That May Make
You Think Twice
About Ever Using a
Cell-Phone Again!

J. WAYNE FRYE

Lynton Buys a New Cell Phone

AND HEARS THE VOICE OF DOOM

A Novella

SAMMY SASQUATCH
AND
THE STS'AILES STAR

A MODERN RETELLING OF THE JOURNEY OF THE THREE WISE MEN
BY
J. WAYNE FRYE

A
Wayne Frye
Book
for
Young Readers

Take a Christmas
Eve journey with
sad, smelly
Sammy
the Sasquatch
and his friends
in search of the
greatest gift of all.

TALES MY GRANDMOTHER TOLD ME

Wayne Frye books for hockey lovers.

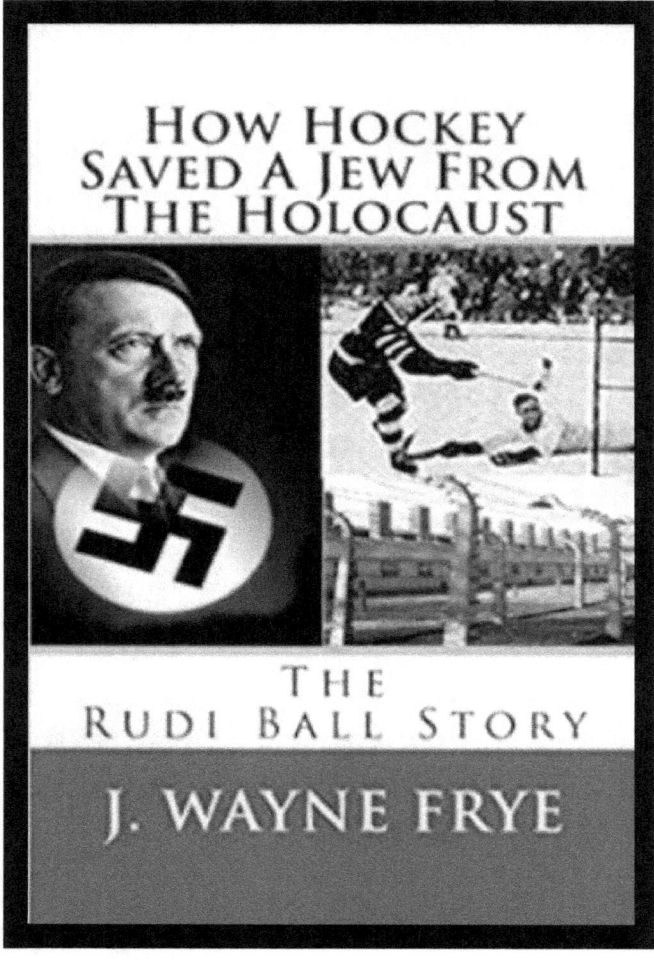

Enjoy hockey combined with romance and mystery
in
Hockey Mania and the Mystery of Nancy Running Elk